RANCHERO

G·K
Hall
&C?

Also by Tom W. Blackburn
in Large Print:

Yanqui

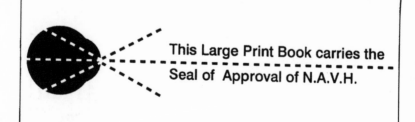

This Large Print Book carries the
Seal of Approval of N.A.V.H.

RANCHERO

Tom W. Blackburn

G.K. Hall & Co. • Thorndike, Maine

Published in 2000 by arrangement with Golden West Literary Agency.

G.K. Hall Large Print Paperback Series.

The text of this Large Print edition is unabridged.
Other aspects of the book may vary from the original edition.

Set in 16 pt. Plantin by Rick Gundberg.

Printed in the United States on permanent paper.

Library of Congress Cataloging-in-Publication Data

Blackburn, Thomas Wakefield.
  Ranchero / Thomas W. Blackburn.
    p. cm.
  ISBN 0-7838-9045-1 (lg. print : sc : alk. paper)
  1. Large type books. I. Title.
  PS3552.L3422 R36 2000
  813′.54—dc21   00-021093

FOR MY SON, JOE
who was, is, and always will be
un gran ranchero

CHAPTER ONE

The bench mark at the southeast corner of the Corona Grant was atop a symmetrical cinder cone called Fire Mountain. The lava malpais which spread across much of the south boundary had spewed from this imposing volcanic fumarole. It was a notable landmark, visible from almost any point on the ranch, and was equally visible from most directions to a big slice of the rest of northcentral New Mexico as well. When it loomed into view, it spelled home. None too soon, this trip.

Spencer Stanton was in a turbulent mood. It had been long building. Irritatingly, there was nothing specific. Only a vague unease, a restlessness for which he could discover no one valid source. An accumulation of small things. A feeling of personal impatience and self-dissatisfaction. So much time passed. So much to do. So little done.

He pulled up at the summit of The Crossing over The Reef to let stock and crew climb up to him. Jim Henry — Jaime, in this Mexican country — Benny and Ramón Archuleta, kids, remote shirttail cousins of 'Mana's family. A hell of a crew. And twenty-two head of beef. All he could find worth having at any price between Bent's Fort on the Arkansas and the head of the Purgatoire. Nothing else to show for a saddle-galling three-hundred-mile ride. A hell of a buying trip.

The climb over The Reef was taxing for driven stock, but the view from the summit of The Crossing was magnificent. Fire Mountain was to the south. To the west the snow-capped wall of the Sangre de Cristos extended from the canyon of the Cimarron to the congestion of big peaks between the Mora Valley and Santa Fe. On the east, broken only by an occasional dry-land butte, was the gently curving horizon-line of the *llanos estacados*. All between was the Corona.

Jaime Henry's horse came to rest of its own accord. Jaime hooked his off knee over the horn of his saddle. He grinned as he always did when some elevation afforded a vista over the ranch.

"Grander and greener, all the time," he gloated.

"Like all those grazing herds of cattle we don't have," Stanton growled wryly.

"Hell of a lot more than you started with," Jaime answered with undiminished pride.

"Damned near ten years."

"Seven. You got a sore ass. What you need is a bottle, a bath, and a bait of 'Mana's cooking."

Jaime stuffed his boots back into his stirrups, stood in them, and called to the Archuleta boys.

"*Vamonos, amigos!* Let's show these critters their new home."

The cattle picked up wearily under the slap of rein ends and took the down-trail into the basin.

Stanton watched Jaime, a man grown, now. He supposed this was a part of what was wrong. He was attached to his *segundo*. But not as he would have been to a son. No man could pretend otherwise without lying to himself in some dark recess.

When he had set out to build the Corona, he had not been building merely for 'Mana and himself. He had not been building for just one generation. Certainly not for a Missouri trail-orphan whom he had picked up from a string of freight wagons on the long road out from the river to Mexican Santa Fe.

He had once had a family. He had once had sons. All no more than deliberately forgotten Virginia memories now. But it looked as if he was to be denied that in New Mexico.

The first time he had slept with her, 'Mana had jokingly accused him of instant fatherhood, pointing to Jaime, then a boy, and Chato, a young Ute of the same age, who had been in their first camp at that time. He and 'Mana did not speak of it now. They had not for a long time. He could not hurt her in that way. But that void was a hard thing to live with.

Nothing a man planned worked out exactly as he dreamed it. In some things there was no second chance.

At the base of The Reef, where The Crossing

9

came down off the great mesa onto Corona grass, the Indian trail they had been following swung westward toward the Cimarron on the old trade road to Taos. A direct but unmarked route to ranch headquarters branched off there.

Absorbed with his thinking and unmindful of his horse, Stanton had let Jaime and the Archuleta boys gain a couple of hundred yards on him with the stock. He kicked up and rounded an outcropping to find all three dismounted, kneeling beside the body of a man half rolled under some brush beside the Corona trail, a few yards off the road to Taos. Jaime rose to face him as he swung down.

"Fergy," he said. "It ain't pretty, Spence."

Stanton pushed past him.

Eli Ferguson was one of those strange men whom the mountains seemed to attract. They were not ambitious, gregarious, adventurer-businessmen like the Bent brothers and Ceran St. Vrain, unabashedly seeking out the Indian trade and seldom working the streams themselves. Their life was among the deep canyons and high peaks. Stanton believed, as well as he could understand the few he had met, they were seeking solitude rather than fortune.

They were loners, disappearing for months at a time with no other human companionship but their own. They hunted only to eat. They took only the finest prime pelts and in no greater amount than necessary to meet their own modest needs for another season.

They came in once or twice a year to Bent's or Taos, often to even more remote posts. Trading done, they disappeared as quietly as they had come. If theirs were the only human tracks along them, the beaver streams would last forever.

Three or four years before, Fergy had stumbled against the stout cottonwood door of the Corona house with a howling, blinding blue norther blizzard at his back, badly frostbitten and half dead. Utterly mortified that he could have lost the way so thoroughly in the storm — any storm in this high country he knew so well — he wanted only a drink, a meal, and to get back onto the Taos road.

'Mana was captivated by his painful embarrassment and gentle, self-effacing manner. She took charge over his protests and nursed him through two months of their hardest winter. When the first spring thaw came, his crippling frostbite had blackened and sloughed away. Reluctantly satisfied he was sufficiently healed to fend for himself again, 'Mana had let him go with a possibles sack sufficient to do him for months.

He was back that fall with the great, thick, soft-tanned grizzly rug that he insisted must lie on 'Mana's side of the bed in the Stanton bedroom. On the next trip he brought her a marvelous Ute-made beaver cap and long coat which she had worn ever since from first snow-fly till the frost was gone.

Now the old man lay here with the whole back

11

of his head crushed by some crude club. Stanton touched the body but could not tell how long he had been dead. No more than a day, he thought. The big black and red ants, the true scavengers of this high country, had not yet found him. It was unquestionably a white man's work. Such men as Fergy were recognized and welcomed everywhere by the tribes. They had no Indian enemies.

Unfortunately, the cattle had passed ahead before the body had been discovered. Tracks and other signs had been obliterated. Fergy's horse and outfit were gone, along with whatever he might have had in his pack. It was a singularly vicious piece of business. Stanton was angered that the first grave on the Corona must be this one. No man should die for so little.

Jaime broke out a saddle shovel and began to dig where the body lay. The Archuleta boys, who had come too lately to the Corona to have known the old mountain man, shaped and set a sapling cross and traced the same symbol across their breasts, hats in hand.

"Go with God," they prayed beneath their breath.

That was what was always said in this country. There were no other words when death struck.

They all mounted up and started the cattle moving again. That, too, was always done in this country. The dead remained behind. The living went on, also hoping beneath their breath that they, too, went with God. 'Mana had tried to explain it. It was the way of life. There could be no lingering. Too many pony tracks in the dust. Too much work to be done. Too many days to pass.

The sun lowered. Shadows reached out from the mountains. By a quirk of terrain, they were into the darkening twilight blanket of one of the big peaks to the west when Jaime suddenly held his hand high, silently halting them. Less than a mile away, still in brilliant sunlight flooding through a notch in the westward mountains, three riders with a single packhorse were coming out of a shallow roll in the grass.

They were on a parallel course, moving in the same direction as the Corona crew, but in a peculiar crisscross pattern. Stanton recognized it at once. So did Jaime.

"Cutting for sign," he said. "Looking for something or somebody. Maybe the way to the house."

Stanton nodded. That, too, was part of his unease. The Archuleta family and old Amelio each occupied one of the snug little adobe houses he had built down by the corrals. The old agreement was still in effect. A smoke by day and a signal fire by night would bring Chato and some of the young Utes down from the mountains in a few hours' time.

But the adobes at the corrals were as distant as the mountain camps of the Utes if the need for help was instant. Stanton had felt growing self-recrimination in this absence. He had left 'Mana

13

with only Amelio to stay at the house with her. Not that the old man wasn't trustworthy. His loyalty was fierce. But he had broken his leg in a horse-fall the previous spring, and it had not healed back strongly enough to wrap a saddle again. Like Eli Ferguson, Amelio had become 'Mana's slave during his convalescence. Quite literally. He had insisted on earning his keep and had since hobbled about the house, sweeping and dusting and scrubbing, hardly letting her out of his sight.

It was utter devotion, but it was not protection. Not the kind which might be needed when the grave of a murdered man lay beside a trail at the foot of The Reef and there were nameless intruders on Corona grass. The grant was no longer the solitary and secure Eden it had been when Spencer Stanton had first ridden onto it in pursuit of some Indian horse thieves.

"Keep the cattle moving," he ordered Benny and Ramón Archuleta. "We'll be late enough getting in as it is."

He signaled Jaime to accompany him and they cut off toward the riders.

Jaime slid his rifle from under his thigh. "Know what I think?" he said.

Stanton knew. Fergy was dead.

"We'll see," he promised.

Because of the varied light and their angle of approach, they rode to within a few rods of the strangers before they were seen. The men were startled by their sudden appearance but seemed neither alarmed nor hostile. They pulled up to wait.

All three were big-bodied and well made. They had good heads, regular features, and an arrogant pride of carriage, even in the saddle, all indicating strong stock somewhere back along the line. But everything else about them betrayed the drifter, the ne'er-do-well, the summer traveler. A glance told Stanton they were without ambition, with pride only in their physical presence. A familiar enough kind where moving men gather. Too damned lazy to work long for an honest wage, too ready to swap or pilfer whatever they could for the next breakfast and the easy life.

He had little fear of such men. They made poor friends but seldom dangerous enemies. Riffraff, they had called them in Virginia and had kept them moving on. These three were unique in only one respect. Their relationship was obvious. Stanton realized at once they were brothers. When he spoke, he held the eyes of all three.

"Looking for something?"

The eldest appeared to be in charge. He glanced around as though puzzled, then seemed to understand the reference was to the crisscross pattern they had been riding. But he did not answer directly. His eyes settled on the rifle across Jaime's thighs.

"You learn him to handle that?" he asked Stanton.

"He was born knowing how," Stanton answered shortly. "Don't make him prove it."

"Then learn him not to point it at me. I got a feeling about that."

Stanton glanced at Jaime, who reluctantly shifted the rifle a little. Stanton met the man's eyes again.

"I asked you a question."

"So you did. And if I could figure where you got a right, you'd get an answer."

"You're on his land," Jaime said.

"All this — that yonder?"

The man's gesture took in the whole of the visible basin.

"All of it," Stanton agreed inflexibly.

"For that little dab of cows?"

The stranger indicated the few head the Archuletas were driving.

"There are a few more."

"We heard this was all greaser country."

"He married one," Jaime snapped. "We don't use that word on this ranch."

"They sure do on the river these days. Everybody says the Mexes are going to lose this country. The Texicans'll see to it. That's why we drifted out this way along the Trail. A look-see at the pickings."

"There aren't any on my land," Stanton said.

"No man's bigger'n his britches, mister."

"Try him," Jaime invited malevolently. "Hell, try me!"

"Ringy, ain't he?" the spokesman asked

Stanton, white teeth showing. "Must not get many strangers through."

"We don't."

"None recent?"

"No."

"All right. Reckon you're entitled. What we was cutting for was a game trail that might lead us to decent water for a change and chance of a pot-shot for supper. We was aiming to lay over for a day or so to grass up our horses and rest our ass-bones."

"We buried a man at the foot of that mesa back there a few hours ago," Stanton said coldly. "A friend. Killed in the last twenty-four hours and his outfit taken."

"No wonder you been so damned hostile! Look at our outfit. No sensible man'd have it, the way it's wore down."

Stanton indicated the led horse.

"I'm looking at the pelts on that pack. Our friend was a trapper."

"Well, we sure as hell ain't. Take a good look if you're a mind. Just a few critters that got in our way, here and there. We skinned 'em out on the off chance they'd trade for a bait of grub or something, somewhere along the line."

Stanton reined over to the packhorse. He fingered a couple of the board-hard small-animal pelts he had seen exposed on the pack. The flaying had been so clumsily and indifferently done that they were next to valueless. No one would eat well or long on what could be had for them in trade. A master mountain man like Eli Ferguson would never have been caught dead with the likes of these in his possession.

Jaime pressed up on the other side. Stanton saw his judgement was the same as his own. But hostile distrust lingered in Jaime's eyes. The spokesman saw this.

"We'll throw her down and spread her out so's you can see what else we're packing, if you want," he offered. "Hardly no trouble, for what there is. We been lighter, but I don't recollect when."

He waited for response but got none. Jaime continued to finger the ragged, filthy skins atop the pack.

"Look, we ain't been near yonder mesa. We turned west off the Trail, looking for kinder country and easier going, but we turned south again when we seen how close we was getting to them mountains. High country like that up there plain ain't for us."

Jaime still wasn't convinced but he shrugged wordlessly when Stanton glanced in question at him. Stanton turned back to the three men and indicated the loom of Fire Mountain.

"Bear for that cinder cone," he directed. "You'll hit good grass and cottonwoods next to sweet water in about five miles. Plenty of down wood, so don't cut any."

He reached back and freed a sack on his cantle. It contained the leavings of a spike buck carcass Jaime had dropped from their last camp

18

on the Purgatoire. He passed it to the nearest brother.

"Pronghorns usually come in to water along there," he continued. "This ought to hold you till you get one. Just be sure it isn't wearing our brand before you knock it down."

"That's neighborly," the spokesman said. "We're obliged."

He nodded to his brothers. They turned their horses toward Fire Mountain. Jaime watched them go.

"Give my eye teeth if they was the ones," he said when they were out of earshot. "I'd a loved to a gut-shot the lot."

Stanton nodded, no more pleased than Jaime.

"We better not mention this at the house."

"Fergy, neither?"

Stanton nodded again.

" 'Mana'll begin to wonder after a while when he don't show up for another visit," Jaime warned.

"Best she doesn't know. For the time being, anyway. Pass the word to Benny and Ramón."

Jaime nodded and they resumed after the cattle.

CHAPTER TWO

About an hour after their encounter with the three drifters, Stanton, Jaime, and the Archuleta boys drove into a bunch of beeves marked with the Crown brand of the Corona. They mingled the weary newcomers from the valleys of the Arkansas and Purgatoire among them and left them there to bed down. Freed of their charges, they kicked up and rode on at a lope. It was well after full dark when they picked up the warm, yellow glow of lamplight in the windows of the Corona house.

Stanton and Jaime dismounted in the yard. The Archuletas took the horses on down to the corrals with them. Stanton expected a wary challenge at this hour and got none. He understood as he hurried uneasily to the door. There was laughter and giggling and such a great stomping around within that it had drowned out the sounds of their arrival. He was displeased that no better watch had been kept.

He tried the latch and it tripped easily, without the resistance of the bar within, which he had ordered to be used at nightfall in his absence. He flung the door open and strode angrily across the sill, rooting in his tracks at the scene before him.

Barefoot, hair and clothing in delicious disarray from the pure exuberance of her efforts, Romana Ruíz Stanton was whirling in a wild, ridiculous dervish dance with hobbling old Amelio. Stanton didn't need to see the half-empty *aguardiente* bottle to which Amelio clung to realize that both were as drunk as trail's-end drovers.

They became aware of him and reeled to a stop.

"El Stallión!" Amelio whooped in greeting.

"Sí," 'Mana giggled. *"El Toro Grande!"*

She ran unsteadily across to Stanton, arms outstretched, laughing at her tipsy clumsiness. Her slender, loosely bodiced, high breasted figure was yearning and her beautiful, flushed face was transported in an urgent, earthy, joyous welcome. But in the perversity of mood and moment, what Spencer Stanton saw was in his memory — the face and figure of another woman with whom he had long shared a bed, faithless, drunken, and wanton.

The sharp, spicy tang of *aguardiente* on 'Mana's breath was explosive fuel to his shock and anger. He only understood that she was making a fool of herself, of him. Making a travesty of what they had here, what they yet planned to build. Tippling like a whore with a hired hand, a useless old pensioner, in her own house.

He cuffed her embrace from him. She staggered back, hurt, stunned, disbelieving. He

21

heard Jaime gasp in the doorway behind him. Then Amelio was at him like a bare-fanged cougar. The half empty bottle of cactus whiskey crashed over the crown of his head. A stout, hide-bottomed chair skidded jarringly into his shins. Another, swept from the floor, swung with furious force into his midsection, buckling him to his knees. He was carried onto his back, half stunned, his shoulders pinned to the stone flagging of his own floor. Amelio was astride him, wickedly posing a sliver of Spanish steel at his throat.

"Fool!" the old man shouted. "Have you no ears? Tonight the whole world is singing. Tell him, *patrona.*"

Stanton saw 'Mana's face above him, stained by his blow. Her eyes were swimming, begging him to understand.

"The time that I could be sure came soon after you left," she said pleadingly. "I tried to wait. But tonight — oh, tonight I couldn't help myself any longer. Tonight I just had to tell someone. You will have your son, *querido.*"

Stanton heard Jaime's long, indrawn breath.

"Well, I'm a son of a bitch!"

Amelio eased his knobby knees from Stanton's pinioned arms and got stiffly and clumsily to his feet.

"*Lo siento, Patrón,*" he murmured contritely, putting his blade away.

Stanton lay spread-eagled, looking up into 'Mana's beseeching face, as comprehension cut

22

through him like a thousand deliciously agonizing knives, severing knots and bonds and doubts, freeing him of restraints which had been binding ever tighter with passing months. He sprang suddenly to his feet in one exultant surge.

"Sorry?" he roared at the apologetic Amelio. "Why, you magnificent old goat, I could damned near kiss you!"

But it was 'Mana he swept into his arms, 'Mana who searched eagerly for his mouth with hers. And when he had let his lips tell her the words he did not know how to say, he barked over his shoulder at Jaime, still standing in the open doorway with a silly grin on his face.

"Damn it, just don't stand there, man! Get the Archuletas. *Niños* and all. We've got some celebrating to do."

Jaime drove eagerly back into the night and his boots pounded off down the yard. Stanton swung 'Mana from her feet and carried her across to one of the chairs Amelio had righted. He sank into this with her in his arms, wordlessly caressing her as he would a child, with hands that seemed suddenly much too large.

When Jaime returned breathlessly with the Archuleta clan excitedly streaming behind him, Amelio had produced another bottle of *aguardiente* and was filling tin cups, which Stanton handed to each guest as they came in the door. 'Mana laughed at his insistent hospitality, but when Benny and Ramón uncertainly took their cups, she protested mildly.

"Really, Spence, they're only boys —"

"The hell you say," Stanton challenged expansively. "If they work for the Corona, they're men enough for me, and they're going to drink to the newest Stanton."

That was one dawn the master of the Corona did not see. Tin cup in hand, he suddenly fell on his face in the dooryard while loudly announcing to the silent world what he was now going to build the Corona into for his New Mexican son. It was a notable speech, if 'Mana later quoted it accurately, a thing of which he was never subsequently quite sure. She was capable of considerable sly malice on occasion.

She told him that it had taken four of them to get him in to bed and that he lay as dead until noon. But he was none the worse for it, except for the snigger in her voice. When he got his boots on and a couple of cups of coffee into his belly, he found the world turned right side up again.

Amelio and Jaime had sensibly cleared out, letting them have the day to themselves. There was much to talk about, much to plan. His first sweeping enthusiasm for this land, this country, was back to full tide. His impatience ran far ahead of him.

They would need more room, now. A second wing to the house, of which they had talked so long, must be got up and sealed before first snow to be ready in the spring. 'Mana would need

24

more fitting inside help than Amelio. Stanton must go to Mora or Taos or even Santa Fe to find just the right woman. Another adobe casa for her and her family must be put up with the others near the corrals.

A chapel, too, if Father Frederico was to be persuaded to cross the mountains from Taos for a suitable christening. And an order for all that 'Mana would need must be got off to the River at once so it could be shipped before winter storms risked shutdown of freight runs on the Santa Fe Trail.

'Mana laughed at how swiftly he counted the months and warned they would pass as slowly as any others. It was a day to be remembered.

Jaime ate supper with Amelio and did not come up to the house until later. He waited his time until he was alone with Stanton on the veranda.

"We branded those new beeves today," he reported. "I rode on out east a ways when we got done. Those drifters you let camp on Conejo Creek sure got a funny way of resting their stock and saddles. They spent the whole day cutting all over hell's half acre. Kept clear of our stock, but they're still looking for something. I'd feel a sight better if I knew what."

Stanton shrugged off the Missourian's concern, his mind on other matters.

"I'll take a look, first minute I get. Tomorrow I want you to take the boys up to an aspen stand and snake us down enough saplings for a new stone-boat. We're going to open up the quarry and cut enough rock out for a new wing to the house."

"*Cualquiera que dice,*" Jaime said. "Whatever you say, Spence. I just don't like the idea of jaspers out there that I don't know."

"Get used to it. There'll be more. We can't keep the whole damned country to ourselves forever."

"Suit me better if we could. Think there's anything to those drifters' talk about Texas making a grab for more land out here?"

"That's something else that'll bear some looking into when we get the chance."

"Wouldn't put it past the bragging bastards."

Jaime went in to bed.

He was gone at daylight into the mountains with the Archuletas, a couple of felling axes, and a string of work ponies to snake down the aspen poles Stanton had ordered. The next day they went out to a free-slabbing sandstone ledge they had discovered on the lip of a nearby arroyo and from which they had taken the stone for the original section of the house. They cut big, solid, uniform blocks and set the Archuletas to dragging them by stone-boat into the yard, stacking them ready for use.

It was three days before Stanton thought again of the drifters camped on his grass. He did so then only because a work team strayed while he was at the house for noon dinner and he and Ramón Archuleta rode after it. The horses were

26

halfway out to Conejo Creek when they overtook them.

Being that close and wanting another hour or two in the saddle after the sweat of breaking out stone, Stanton sent Ramón back with the strays and rode on to the place he had given the strangers permission to camp. The three brothers were gone, but there was ample evidence of their stay.

Rather than walk a few yards from their fire to gather the dry deadfall litter which always accumulated under established cottonwoods, they had cut living willow on the creekbank for fuel. The air stank with the remnant carcasses of two pronghorn antelope from which only the best cuts had been taken, leaving the unskinned remains to rot on the ground. There was a broadcast litter of leavings, among which were two empty, labeled bottles of Missouri whiskey. What caught Stanton's eye was another empty bottle, unlabeled, crude, slightly misshapen. He recognized its source at once.

It had been hand-blown by Indians taught the art by Simeon Turley, an enterprising Yankee who had settled on the other side of the mountains at Arroyo Hondo, above Taos. He used these crude homemade containers to dispense the favorite fortifier of the southern trapping trade — the clear, colorless, formidable Taos Lightning he brewed in a distillery attached to his corn fields and grist mill.

No mountain man's pack or possibles bag was complete without an emergency supply. Most maintained it was indispensable, a sure cure for every ill and accident to which man is heir. Eli Ferguson had been one of Turley's most ardent customers. Stanton sent the bottle rolling with the toe of his boot.

It could have been picked up anywhere. It was a standard staple of trade at Taos and Bent's and Santa Fe. Most eastbound freighters carried a ration of Turley's whiskey to wet down the dry crossing between the Canadian and the Arkansas. There was no way this discarded bubble of flawed glass could reasonably be connected with Fergy Ferguson's death.

Nevertheless, Stanton remembered the stubborn doubt which had still plagued Jaime as little as a few days ago. They had, he knew, made a mistake. They should have taken the three brothers up on their offer to open their pack for inspection. At least they would have been sure. Both of them.

Stanton remounted and found to his surprise that departure tracks from the littered campsite led due west, almost on a direct line for the Corona headquarters, rather than east or south as he would have automatically supposed. He kicked up and followed them curiously.

The westerly direction held, but the makers of the tracks had obviously been keeping to lowest possible ground, avoiding visible exposure in the direction of the house and any activity in its vicinity. His curiosity increased. In a couple of miles the tracks tipped into a shallow dry wash and turned abruptly south along its course, joining and intermingling with those of three other southbound horses.

Remembering Jaime's report of the wide riding the drifters had done while supposedly in the rest camp he had permitted them, Stanton thought at first they had meant to double over their own earlier sign. But after he had dismounted and made careful comparison, he realized that the underlying set of tracks had been made by three entirely different animals than the four he had been following.

By the drift of dust in the prints, the comparative dryness of occasional dung-drops, and the spring-back of scuffed clumps of bunch-grass, he judged the second set of tracks had been made considerably earlier than those he had followed down from Conejo Creek. Perhaps several days earlier. He knew, then, that this was what the three brothers had been searching for on his grass. There were other unannounced strangers on the Corona.

It seemed likely the trio he and Jaime had encountered had been trailing these others. Possibly for some time. Certainly a distance as far as from the freight-ruts of the Trail, forty miles or more to the east. They had apparently lost them, searched, and now found them again. If so, there still might be an answer to what had happened to Eli Ferguson at the foot of The Reef.

Stanton pulled up in indecision. He had his belt gun but not his rifle. He didn't relish closing in at short range in an uncertain situation. He would have preferred to turn back for Jaime and the Archuleta boys and their father, Raul. All handled long guns well. But the smell of rain had been in the air since first light this morning, and the mutter of distant thunder back in the mountains had begun to sound occasionally while they were still at the house for the noon meal.

Most storms built against the western slope of the Sangre de Cristos, but once they crested the peaks, showers came swiftly if infrequently down onto the grass at this season. They were usually of short duration and brought only a mild drenching which did not interfere with work afoot and dried in a few minutes. But while it rained, it rained like hell, washing grass and gravel clean of any signs of passage but the deep-worn ruts of old and much used trails.

He reluctantly elected to ride on alone, following the dual tracks south toward Fire Mountain and the badlands of lava malpais which had spewed from it. Tracking became more difficult as he entered the malpais. Pockets of sand and clay, recording passage clearly, became less and less frequent. He had to cast about more often to regain the trail when he lost it. He thought the lead party had taken some pains to conceal its course, inasmuch as was possible without undue loss of time and mileage. The three following did not seem so concerned.

Black thunderheads reared up in the saddles between the backbone peaks of the Sangre de

Cristos and tumbled over, rolling swiftly down the canyons. Thunder cannonaded, echoing and re-echoing in their narrow confines. A fresh westerly wind arose and the lowering clouds began to drape in sheets which shortly obscured the mountains. Lightning flickered through them as the first clouds swept out across the grass toward him.

The distinct, faintly unpleasant odor of ozone was in the air. The mane of his horse, roached short for a few inches ahead of his saddlebow, and the hair at the back of his own neck, separated and stood erect, faintly crackling to the touch with spontaneous electrical discharge.

Stanton relished such high-country manifestations of the tremendous power nature generated in the mountains. They were wild and boisterous and boastful. He thought they were responsible for the thunderous high spirits and exaggerated braggadocio of some who had sought out this country and had been long and lovingly exposed to it, whenever they were themselves at play. Men emulating the land.

Although a woman of great gentleness, pride, and regal decorum, there was much of this in 'Mana, equally a portion of her heritage. A lusty outpouring which on occasion could not be contained. He smiled at certain recollections.

Lightning began to strike and bounce on the open grass, doing no harm but to make his horse flinch and to awe the senses. By the rule of thumb of ten miles to the counted minute be-

31

tween the flash of the bolt and the ensuing peal of thunder, he measured his distance from the advancing, turbulent front of the shower.

When it was little more than a mile away, the tracks he was following entered a passage between two dikes of slickrock lava. The first drops caught him here and he broke out his slicker. The rain came in a sheet, drumming on the brim of his hat and rattling the stiff oilskin in which he had wrapped himself.

It was over nearly as quickly as it had come. Less than five minutes from first drop to last. The front swept on swiftly to the south and east, obscuring the loom of Fire Mountain as it went. The sun broke through behind the storm, revealing the mountains to the west in a fresh-washed silhouette.

But in that short time, every vestige of the tracks he had been following had melted away, including the fresh markings of his own horse. However, the sign had led in here and the wet slickrock on either side would have been impossible to climb out over even dry, so he held on, knowing any who had passed ahead would have had to do the same.

It was in this way that he found another campsite. In about a quarter of a mile the flanking dikes separated to form a little grassed bowl in the malpais, four or five acres in extent. The site was more littered than the one on Conejo Creek had been. But it appeared equally deserted. Except for one thing.

A single cottonwood stood in the center of the bowl beside the pool of a small spring which watered it well. The tree was quite large for its kind at this altitude. A heavy horizontal limb spread pleasant shade and shelter over a small patch of summer soft-grass as densely tufted and green as a tended lawn. The camp fire-circle was in the center of this.

Above it, hanging by the neck from the sheltering limb on a length of rope, the body of a man was swinging slightly in the dying wind.

CHAPTER THREE

Stanton rode cautiously on in. There was no challenge. He cut the body down and dismounted to examine it. It was in frightful shape, battered and swollen beyond recognition. The man had not died by the rope about his neck. He had been ruthlessly and thoroughly beaten to death beforehand. Stanton thought the shocking cadaver had been hanging in the wind for several days.

He made a slow foot-circuit of the bowl. The bloated carcasses of two poor, travel-gaunted saddle horses lay shot in a cul de sac. Nearby, a big fire had been built against a lava run. Judging by the charred remnants, everything flammable in the camp had been burned.

There were the shattered remains of two more of Simeon Turley's crude Taos Lightning bottles. Pots, pans, and some tin utensils lay scattered about, smashed beyond usability as though hit with the flat of an ax. A dung heap of horse-dropping and big-boweled human feces lay on the clean black sand at the bottom of the shallow little spring, scumming its surface.

There were several possible exits from the bowl. Stanton checked them all. The brief rain had washed the record as clean as though none had ever existed. Remounting, he rode a wider circle with the same result.

He had no doubt this was the work of the three drifters he had followed. Tracks and timing made that almost certain. They had found their quarry and the Corona would have its second grave. But there had been three horses in the party they were tracking. Allowing for a pack-horse, there must have been at least one other man in this camp when they came upon it.

They could have carried him away. Or he had escaped his companion's fate and crawled off into the malpais to hide or die. That would account for the destruction of horses and equipment. And the deliberate fouling of the spring, so the missing man could not survive, should he return after the killers were gone.

Stanton hallooed, fired three quick shots from his handgun, and hallooed again. Echoes were the only response. He waited until the last died and reloaded, cursing softly, before he set about the only thing left to be done.

The ground was too hard for digging. He dragged the dead man to a collapsed tube-bubble left in the flowing lava when it cooled. Lowering the body into this natural vault, he rolled heavy, weather-riven chunks of the glassy black stone in to seal it from disturbance.

Bending low to dislodge a last stubborn chunk of loosened lava, he found himself peering past it into a small, horizontal chamber which had escaped his notice on his feet. Eyes peered back at him. Fearful wild animal eyes, set in the face of a woman. He rolled the rock away and came to his feet, so as not to alarm her further.

"It's all right, now," he said quietly. "You're safe."

The woman slowly wriggled from her hiding place. A girl, really, he saw. It seemed impossible that she could have compressed her body into so small a space. She was thin, ragged, barefoot, and scarcely more than half clad. What remnants she wore were rain-wet and plastered uncompromisingly to her skin. She shivered as the lowering sun touched her.

Her hair hung in a colorless tangle. Her face was bruised and cut by the sharp stone of the cramped shelter. Her hands were rough and bore more cuts and scratches from the lava. Her feet had been cut unmercifully by the razor-sharp obsidian chips everywhere underfoot in the malpais. The wounds had begun to fester for want of attention.

Only her eyes betrayed her youth. They were well spaced, unusually large and clear, and a luminously deep-violet. But when Stanton looked into them, they told him nothing. There was a translucent defensive screen within their depths beyond which he could not penetrate.

"Are you all right?" he asked gently.

She looked down at herself, shrugged, and nodded.

"Who are you?"

"Helga."

"No other name?"

She shook her head. Realizing what she must have been through, Stanton did not press but continued his effort to reassure her.

"I'm Spencer Stanton, a rancher north of here."

She nodded again.

"We saw your place. I wanted to stop, but Jake said we couldn't risk it."

"Your husband?"

"That son of a bitch? He was as rotten as any of them."

"I've been following the tracks of three men and a packhorse. It looked like they might have been trailing you."

"For weeks," the girl assented wearily.

"Three brothers?"

She closed her eyes as though to shut something out, then reopened them.

"Mine."

Stanton was incredulous.

"Yours? Are you trying to tell me that they did this? In God's name, why?"

"Because I run off with Jake and a poke of gold they took from a bank on the river. Jake and me ain't what galled their guts. It was the eighteen hundred dollars in the poke that brung them after us."

"They beat him to death for that?"

"Would me, too, if I hadn't hid when I heard them coming. As it was, before they left they sure fixed it so's I couldn't get out of here on my own."

"How long ago?"

"Two days. Three. How do I know, now?"

She began to shiver again, uncontrollably.

Stanton was contrite. "Wait here. I'll get my horse."

He crossed the bowl with quick strides and rode back. He handed her down his slicker. It was a chill enough comfort but some protection against the evening breeze beginning to build from the mountains.

"We'll get you back to my wife as fast as possible," he promised.

She pulled the slicker on and clumsily hooked up the clasps. He reached down a hand. She swung up behind him, locking her arms about him for balance. He put the horse in motion.

He could feel the violently shivering tremors of her body as they rode. He regretted he had not had a warmer jacket on his saddle. Easing up the tail of his shirt at the sides, he thrust her rough little hands through the openings. She clutched gratefully at the warmth of his body.

As her hands warmed, her shivering gradually subsided. She leaned warily forward, flattening her cheek against his shoulder blade. He thought she slept. But after a mile or two she suddenly spoke wistfully.

"Will I have a bed?"

Stanton was startled from his own thoughts. "Hunh?"

"In that fine red stone house of yours."

"Sure," he agreed. "It won't be long now."

"Good." She sighed long and deeply. "Been a mighty far spell since I slept in an honest-to-God bed."

She replaced her cheek. Another mile or two passed and they emerged from the malpais onto the better going of open grass. Stanton knew she must be bone-tired, exhausted and utterly wrung out. Again he thought she slept. But again she stirred.

"Funny how it works out," she said in a voice so faint and small he could barely hear her above the sounds of motion. "We knowed they'd follow. But the horses was fresh and we had plenty grub in our kit. It'd take them three or four days to sober up and stagger back from town and find out what we'd done. So we had a good start and plenty of country to put between them and us. We figured we'd be safe in Santa Fe or some greaser place down this way —"

"Forget it for now," Stanton advised. "Take it easy. You can tell us about it, later."

She didn't seem to hear him.

"It was the dry crossing below the Arkansas that broke our pick. Jake was no good in country like that. When we hit water again our horses and kit was used up and so were we. Sante Fe was too far, but we heard there was a shorter trail over the mountains to a place called Taos —"

Stanton stiffened. "You took the Taos road?"

"Started to, but I caught the gripe. Had to stop ever little while. I was out in the brush like that when a horse come along easy the other

39

way. When I got back it was standing with ours and Jake was tearing open the pack on its back. I could see some good furs and a kit that'd take us a sight further than Santa Fe if need be. I didn't see the old man on the ground till I almost stepped on him."

"Wearing buckskin?" Stanton asked quietly. "A mountain man? A trapper?"

The girl sat up involuntarily. "How'd you know?"

"The furs."

"Know who he was, too, don't you?"

"A friend. We found the body."

"Jesus!" the girl breathed. "Then you seen what Jake had done to him. He had to slap me around good afore I came back to my senses. After that — well, like he said, it was done. The pack was ours for the taking. Even I didn't want no part of them mountains if we didn't have to. So we turned down here to hole up and they caught up with us."

She slumped forward again and her cheek came back against his shoulder blade.

"I'm sick-sorry about your friend, mister," she said miserably. "I don't know what to say."

"Nothing," Stanton advised bleakly. "Forget it if you can. The whole thing."

They rode on in silence. Presently their approach was seen at a distance from the house. Jaime and the Archuletas had brought in the last boat of rock for the day. The boys were on their way down to the corrals with the red, sandstone-dusted work teams. Jaime and 'Mana waited on the veranda. Jaime came out to the horse as Stanton pulled up to the dooryard.

'Mana took one look at the girl as Jaime helped her down and came at an anxious half-run to solicitously aid her toward the house. The girl made a strong, prideful effort to walk upright and steady, without flinching, but Stanton saw the pus marks her lacerated bare feet left as she crossed the veranda flagging with 'Mana. So did Jaime.

"I need a drink," Stanton told him.

Jaime called into the house. *"Amelio, una bebida para el patrón, por favór!"*

The old man appeared in the doorway with a bottle. Stanton absently wiped the neck with the heel of his hand and took a long pull. It did nothing for him. The taste in his mouth would take many such swallows to burn out.

He handed the bottle to Jaime, who took a thoughtful sip, his eyes never leaving Stanton's face.

"So they finally found who they were looking for," he said.

Stanton nodded.

"In the malpais. Almost to Fire Mountain. She hid or they'd have found her, too."

"Gone?"

"Long gone. Clean, after that washdown this afternoon. Nothing left but her. But they did us one turn, *amigo*."

Jaime looked at him questioningly, waiting.

41

"They hanged the bastard who killed Fergy."

The Missourian silently took his long pull from the bottle then, and they went into the house together. Both knew it was something they could no longer keep from 'Mana. It would take their combined courage to tell her that in the midst of the greatest happiness of her life, death had come to the Corona.

CHAPTER FOUR

Jaime's things were piled hastily on the long hide settee before the fireplace in the big living room which was also kitchen and dining room. 'Mana had put the girl from the malpais in the room at the far end in which Jaime had slept since the house was roofed, dispossessing him without even a by-your-leave. Stanton was displeased. The girl was no permanent part of the Corona, as Jaime had always been, and he did not see the necessity. But Jaime was not distressed. He gathered up his belongings.

"I'll bunk with Amelio," he told Stanton. "Be back directly."

He carried his possessions out into the night. Stanton had another drink, still from the neck of the bottle. There was no more civilized way to absorb the ardor of *aguardiente*. Its fire defied the niceties of tumbler and cutting water. Amelio paraded importantly back and forth, carrying buckets of hot water into the room where 'Mana worked with Helga, in the process emptying the reservoir of the patent cooking stove Stanton had shipped out from St. Louis the past season.

The strong odor of a healing unguent the Utes made from mountain laurel filled the air when-

43

ever the door to the room was open. And 'Mana's voice, soft and comforting, could be heard. Jaime returned and had another drink with Stanton. Finally, first ministrations were over and 'Mana joined them.

"She's sleeping," she reported. "Too tired to even eat. But she'll be all right. You'll see, tomorrow. She's as starved down as your Yankee beeves were when they first came to water here."

"There was no need to move, Jaime," Stanton growled.

"It's all right, I tell you, Spence," the Missourian said good-naturedly. "It's the first time I've had a woman in my bed. You wouldn't beat me out of that, would you?"

"We could have rigged a cot out here. It's only for a few days."

"With you men traipsing in and out at all hours?" 'Mana protested.

"I don't imagine that would trouble her all that much," Stanton observed drily.

"I'm surprised at you, Spence," 'Mana said sharply. "She's just a child. A hurt, sick, scared child. Can you believe it? I asked her how old she is. She doesn't know, for sure. She thinks nineteen. Only nineteen!"

Stanton was startled in spite of himself and he saw Jaime's interest sharpen. His own vague personal guess would have missed by nearly a decade.

"Leave the poor dear to me," 'Mana continued firmly. "It's a woman's affair and this is one

44

time we'll do as I say. Now, tell me what happened out there."

Stanton was explicit. So was Jaime in what he could add. What was to be in the open among them must be fully so. To their surprise, 'Mana took the news of Fergy's death, and the violence which had been done in the malpais, sadly but calmly.

"Men die here," she said, instinctively reverting to Spanish as she often did when weighty matters were afoot. "Many have. Many more will. Women, too. The three of us, in our time. My whole family, one by one if you remember. Long before you came. Once upon a time neighbors. Old friends. Enemies. It's always been like that here. It always will be. I'll miss Fergy. I'll miss him terribly. But I can't grieve for him."

Stanton shook his head, marveling, realizing again that he could never match her serenity of spirit. She could be a tigress, on occasion, but never out of inner conflict. Only in defense of that which she loved. The changelessness of this country had permeated the marrow of her bones and the depths of her soul.

It was primitive — primordial. The Utes had this same timeless taproot in the land. The Taoseños, the Pueblos, the Apache and Navajo. This oneness with the mountains and the high grass and the desert. This brotherhood with all that lived and grew and died upon them. God in nature.

It was almost impossible for one of his blood and tradition to achieve it or even really understand. The faiths were too faint, the restlessness too compelling, the drives too irrepressible, the values too finite. To live was not enough. To do was all-important. Even the Bible preached God in self. There was no place for permanence and peace. Too much was to be won.

'Mana saw the depth of his thought and misunderstood.

"But I do grieve over something else," she went on. "Worry's a better word. Something I've been afraid of for a long time. Since you first came here, *querido*. And you, Jaime. Sol Wetzel and some of the other foreigners now rooted in Santa Fe. Simeon Turley at Arroyo Hondo. Carson at Taos. The Bents and St. Vrains. Yes, even Fergy, himself, I suppose."

Stanton started to explain what he had really been thinking. She silenced him with a gesture.

"Oh, it's not you who worry me," she protested. "Any of you. You were the first ones. You all belong to us, now, as you two belong to me — to the Corona. You belong to this New Mexico of ours."

She leaned over and took Stanton's hand earnestly. Then, in inclusive afterthought, Jaime's as well.

"What I'm afraid of are these new ones who are beginning to come after. That poor girl in there. Her beastly brothers. The scoundrel who helped her run away. The men and wagons

46

rolling down the Trail to Santa Fe, these days. Who do they belong to? What will the end be?

"Every *paisano*, every *vaquero*, the smallest farmer on the *milpas* knows by this time that these outlanders want this country, too. But it's different with them. They don't love it as we do."

She paused and looked searchingly at them both.

"I don't know how to say what it is that I'm afraid of. It's ugly. I guess rape's the only word a woman can use."

"You expect me to do something to stop it?" Stanton asked, beginning to understand.

'Mana nodded earnestly.

"Before it's too late."

He was wryly amused by her boundless faith in his ability to do all things.

"What, in God's name?" he challenged.

"More than cut stone and build extra rooms we don't absolutely have to have, right now. I know you think all that's for me — for the child. But face it, Spence. It's actually for yourself — for your own vanity. Spencer Stanton — *El Señor, El Patrón, El Ranchero Grande*."

She impatiently silenced him again as he started to protest.

"I know. Yesterday I shared it all with you. Yesterday I humored you as you've always humored me. Yesterday I was excited and happy and had no fears. But new stone walls won't hold back the inevitable, Spence. Not after today."

47

He squeezed her hand, smiling tolerantly.

"Whoa, now! It isn't all that grim. You're upset over Fergy — over what happened to that poor, mistreated little tramp in there. Tomorrow the sun will be shining again. We'll finish the house."

She stood up.

"All right, Spence," she said. "It's your ranch." Her hand touched the flat of her belly. "It's your son."

Jaime was scrounged down long on the settee, thumbs hooked in front pants pockets and boots thrust far out before him. His glance flicked thoughtfully up to Stanton as he, too, came to his feet.

"She may be right," the Missourian said quietly. "We been keeping our nose to the grindstone pretty steady and we don't get wind of much way up here. Remember what one of that girl's brothers said when we stopped them out there above Conejo Creek? Talk they'd heard on the river? Us New Mexicans just could be half whipped and not even know it."

"Oh, hell, now," Stanton protested, "I can't take on the both of you! Lord knows I've learned that."

He put his arm around 'Mana.

"You're a hard-headed, spoiled-rotten woman," he continued. "But if you're actually that worried, I'll haul my butt down to Santa Fe. I can at least get our business done there while I'm about it. If there's any trouble with these stragglers drifting in, I'll find out about it. Maybe we can do something if we have to."

'Mana turned her face up eagerly to him.

"When will you go, Spence? When?"

"Well, tomorrow be all right? Or do you want me to start right now?"

She smiled sheepishly and shook her head.

"Too late, tonight. You haven't had your supper."

She moved off to help Amelio set and serve the meal simmering on the stove. Stanton hauled Jaime to his feet and punched a finger against the middle button of his shirt.

"Just between us, *amigo*," he said quietly, "I expect to see those new walls up and timbered when I get back."

Jaime glanced across at 'Mana, bustling about the kitchen.

"You expect a hell of a lot," he complained.

After Jaime and Amelio had gone down to the adobes and 'Mana had turned in, Stanton made up his saddle kit for the ride to Santa Fe, using the kitchen table as a place to assemble it. It amused him to note by the collection how rapidly a man adjusted to this country.

There were great distances here, often deceptive in both space and time, and a long rider must be prepared for them. But even essentials soon become non-essential. Bulk and weight became critical. In time a man learned that the land was not as harsh as it seemed. Sustenance and even comfort could usually be had without difficulty if he was not overburdened. A traveler could be judged by the bulk of the roll on his saddle and the sheen of his horse's hide.

He banked the kitchen fire in ash for the night and was about to turn in himself when he remembered something he needed to know. He crossed to the door at the far end of the room and entered softly without knocking, closing the door behind him. The powerful, astringent odor of 'Mana's Ute unguent was strong in the room, cleansing the lungs like the smoke of a laurel fire.

A small, pebble-glass night lamp atop the towering, chestlike Spanish *vargueño,* which had come from 'Mana's now abandoned family adobe, was trimmed as low as the wick would go. Stanton crossed to the bed. Even in this faint light he could see that 'Mana had done much for this girl who had crawled out from under the lava at his feet.

She slept peacefully. With her hair brushed, her features cleansed and treated and in repose, her slender body under the smooth-drawn coverlet limp with the total relaxation of exhaustion, she looked the child 'Mana had called her. All knowingness and fear and desperation were washed away. Stanton turned back a corner of the covering and gripped her shoulder firmly and shook her.

She responded slowly, softly whimpering in faintest protest. Her eyes opened and focused on him. It took a little time for rationality to dawn. She reached up and took his hand from her shoulder, so close to the young breast beneath, and carried his fingers to her lips. She kissed them.

"I didn't thank you," she sighed.

"Can you hear me?" he whispered. "Can you understand?"

"I've never known a woman like her," she murmured. "Not close enough to talk to and smell. Close enough to even touch and her touch me."

Stanton's hand returned to her shoulder and he shook her again, gently.

"Listen to me, Helga. I have to know. It may be important. To others if not to me. What are their names?"

Her hand sleepily covered his, pressing it against her. Her eyes closed.

"Names? Who?"

"Your brothers."

A tremor shook her but her eyes did not reopen.

"Cagle," she whispered, almost soundlessly. "Matt and Zeke and Lew."

Stanton waited to see if there was more, but her breathing deepened and he realized she slept again, as quickly as that. It was all right. It was enough. Perhaps more than he'd ever need. He was sorry to have disturbed her, even this little, but it was better now than at the early hour of his departure, and he had to know this much, should he ever encounter them again. He with-

51

drew his hand and replaced the coverlet. She was smiling faintly in her sleep as he turned away.

He undressed in the warmth of the banked kitchen fire and blew out the lamp in the big room. When he went in and slid into bed beside 'Mana and drew her to him, she stirred sleepily.

"How is she?" she asked.

Stanton realized that the odor of the Ute ointment had clung to him. She was not an easy woman to mislead, even in small things. He smiled to himself.

"Sleeping like a baby," he said.

CHAPTER FIVE

Stanton supposed he owed the courtesy of a call at Don Felipe Peralta's Rancho Mora after so long a time between visits. Mora, a day and half to the south, was the Corona's closest neighbor. Don Felipe had long been 'Mana's confidant and, after the death of the last of her people, her guardian. He would be delighted with her news and the prospect of an heir on the Corona.

In addition, Stanton's personal private highroad to Santa Fe lay on that side of the basin, a little known Indian trail over the awesome heights of El Cumbre Pass, which dropped swiftly down the west slopes of the Sangre de Cristos into the capital at a saving of many miles and hours in the saddle. But he thought that both Don Felipe and El Cumbre could wait for the return trip.

He wanted to determine before reaching Santa Fe just how much justification, aside from their own recent experiences on the Corona, actually existed for the fears 'Mana had communicated to him. As a result, he rode into the dawn, leaving the silent house behind him, on a wide-swinging detour which skirted the malpais out eastward of the cone of Fire Mountain.

He was surprised to find stock sign, certainly

his own, out as far as twenty miles, where there was usually poor grass and scant water at this time of year. He thought that upon his return they would have to start putting more miles under their saddles to prevent this unnecessary scattering. Not yet was the Corona in any danger of overgrazing closer in. But it was good to see the whole of the ranch was enjoying a green season, compared to the country north of The Reef.

This bunch had apparently grazed only briefly here and then worked back toward better forage closer to the mountains, but he found one animal which had not. It was a fairly recent cougar kill, notable for how far the big cat had dragged the carcass of its victim to find a feeding place which suited its fancy. He thought the yearling it had taken might have weighed four hundred pounds on the hoof, but the drag marks extended for nearly a quarter of a mile. It was an unusual demonstration of the lion's power and finicky arrogance.

As always, he regretted the loss of even a single head of stock, unable to accept even natural attrition. But the cougar had apparently been migrating across this poorer country or it would not have taken a beef. Like the hunting Indians, most predators in this country disdained domestic kills where wild game was plentiful. For this reason, he and Jaime had from the beginning tried to avoid disturbing native herds and habits wherever possible.

The grass continued to thin out onto the

llanos as he rode on eastward. In late afternoon he crossed the cutbank red run of the Canadian and reached the Santa Fe Trail just above Taylor Springs. This was his first objective and he was astonished at the physical change in the Trail since he had last seen it.

Although normally dry, the turf here in natural state had the accumulated spring of centuries of growth and sodding. He remembered how even the broad tires of the freight wagon he had brought down here with his first few pitiful cattle had cut deeply across virgin patches. Drivers had quickly learned to track each other exactly to take advantage of the compacting of those ahead. The result had been a dual ribbon across the grass from which choking dust arose as the sod wore away. These dusty tracks, hard-packed beneath the surface, made far easier going for the straining spans than the uncut sod.

But now, after only these few years, the ribboned tracks had broadened into a great roadway, wide enough in most places for opposing wagons to pass and cut two to four feet and more beneath the original level. Generally following contours and detouring only where the original line cut across natural drainage, inviting washouts, it was visible to the horizon in either direction. So deeply cut, a scar would remain in places across the land for all time to come.

Stanton knew 'Mana had been right in one thing, at least. There was plainly more traffic over this highway of commerce to Mexican

Santa Fe these days than he could ever have believed when he made the crossing. There were far more Yankees streaming in than he had realized in the isolation of the Corona. It was a sobering recognition and justified his long detour.

He rode on down to a large, much used campground beside the Trail and was pleased to see that he would have it to himself. The springs here were the first sweet water after the dry crossing down from the Arkansas, the section of the Trail sometimes known as the *jornada del muerte*. It had been an important watering place to the horse Indians and those before them, centuries before the first wagons.

In those days, Chato and the Utes claimed, the springs were important for more than first potable water after the desert of the *jornada* and the alkaline flats of the Staked Plains. There were beds of both fine flint and obsidian nearby, so they had been the site of an ancient armory as well.

Since childhood, riding the Corona in the days her people had held the grant, 'Mana had collected the stone implements of the Indians and their ancestors, the *anasazi,* the ancient ones. Often as she rode with Stanton, even now, she would pull up and excitedly jump down to retrieve a perfect arrow point or a fist-sized *mano* or a small, bowl shaped *metate* from the rubble of an arroyo floor.

The favorites in her collection were tiny, perfectly chipped and shaped arrow points which

Chato said were bird points, used with light arrows for the smallest game. 'Mana had a different explanation. Notwithstanding the authority of Chato's Ute heritage, she maintained they were toys, painstakingly chipped in diminutives of war and hunting tips by patient and devoted elders to teach the young necessary skills at an early age.

She was proud of her collection and Stanton had always meant to bring her here in hope of adding to it. He didn't know what chance he had of finding anything now after the hundreds, perhaps thousands, of wagons which had camped here, but after he had unsaddled and hobbled his horse, he prodded idly about in more recent litter with a stick.

In a few minutes, on the edge of a diminutive cutbank, he had the good luck to break into the tell-tale gray ash layering of a much older camp midden. Scattered through it were a great many flakelike, small, crescent-shaped flint and obsidian pressure chips and a few half-formed pieces which had been abandoned because of flaws where the chipping process had gone wrong.

But there were perfect points in the detritus as well. At the end of half an hour he had a handful of assorted arrowheads and two fine spear points, each several inches long and unlike any he had ever seen before. He knew 'Mana would be pleased and wrapped them carefully. He would have to return with her for a more painstaking search.

He cleared a small space of litter beside the largest spring where some unused wood was gathered. Building a fire with it, he made and ate his meal. Then, as full, moonless dark came, he slipped the hobbles and brought his horse in close, picketing it securely. With a caution which had long since become automatic and habitual in the open, he rolled into his blankets some distance from the ebbing fire. Night sounds were reassuring and in minutes he was asleep.

He awakened to the sudden, sure knowledge that he was no longer alone. There had been no hail, no sound of approach. Not even the faint beat a man who literally slept with his ear to the ground could sense from the hoofs of even a walking horse. All night sounds, even the smallest, had ceased. Nature, too, sensed an alien presence. And it was hostile.

No friendly traveler rode in to a night-camp fire in this country without ample warning of his coming. It was too easy a way to get himself shot. Stanton lay motionless, keeping his breathing deep and steady, his eyes on the still glowing embers of his fire.

Presently a shadow moved between Stanton and the fire-glow. The ill-defined shadow of a stalking man, revealed but for an instant. Whoever he was, he was no heavy-footed bush-popper. He was moving like a cat with a consummate skill probably acquired as did a cat by many a night stalk such as this. From the angle of movement, Stanton knew his horse had been found, so the stalker knew he was alone. But he didn't believe his bedground had yet been located.

Very slowly he eased his blankets aside for instant freedom of motion. Very slowly he eased his belt gun from its holster, thumb on the hammer. But he did not ear it to cock, knowing the faint click of the sear would betray him. He lay there on his back, his head slightly raised and his body tensed for the warning, listening with an intensity which made him sweat.

Some men had a scent which was not the odor of an unwashed body. It was an animal thing which was sensed rather than smelled. This one had it. A signal of malevolent presence as unmistakable as that which makes a dog at bay know a man who fears it. Some said that was a scent, too. If so, it was of the same kind. It gave Stanton a direction of approach and warned him the man was very close, now. He could not tell if there were others and did not dare divert his attention.

He forced himself to wait to an unbearable last instant, then he snapped into a sitting position, jerking his knees up against his chest to get his feet under him and to make himself as small a target as possible, there on the ground. In the same moment, over his knees, he fired two of the precious loads in his gun so swiftly that the sound was as of one. But in the instant between them, the flash of the first revealed the silhouette of the stalker, his own gun at ready, not six feet away, and the second shot went home.

Stanton heard the ball strike the man's body as he dove aside in a tumbling roll which brought him to his feet in a crouch, a few yards away. As he fell, the stalker's gun fired into Stanton's blankets and almost instantly, from divergent angles across the camp, two more guns fired at the double flash which remained on the retinas of their owners' eyes, the shot where Stanton's gun had been a moment earlier.

Stanton remained frozen where he was. He beard a gasping grunt of pain from near his blankets. Then came the sound of movement with no attempt to conceal it. He realized the man he had shot was painfully dragging himself to his feet. He rested a moment to steady himself, then went staggering blindly off toward the fire, careless of noise.

"All right?" a voice called sharply.

"No, God damn it!" the wounded man groaned. "Where are you? The son of a bitch nailed me."

"Stay away from that light!" another voice warned. And then, "Jesus, you're bleeding. Let's get to hell out of here."

Sound receded. In a few minutes Stanton heard horses. They passed far out on the grass. The hoofbeats faded off to the north, paralleling the Trail. He went to the fire and cautiously kicked it up for light. There was no challenge. As soon as he was saddled and had his kit up, he doused the flames with water, refilled his canteen, and took the Trail southward.

It was as dark a night as he could remember, a thing for which he was grateful, but it made difficult going, now. However, once he was out from under the cottonwoods shading Taylor Springs, one of the unusual phenomena of this high country came to his aid.

Some color quality in the gray-green of the grass seemed to take on a kind of luminescence from starshine alone, multiplying that faint light so that he only had to stay on turf to clearly see obstacles. Presently, when his eyes became accustomed to the effect, silhouettes and the bold mountain and mesa patterns of the horizon line also appeared. Thereafter, it was easy enough riding and he let his horse pick its own way.

Stanton had just breakfasted at a leisurely midmorning rest stop on a *rillito* under the stark, looming mesa of Wagonmound when half a dozen riders came up fast from the south. There were three kinds of horsemen in this country. Each was distinctive and readily identifiable from a distance.

Indians rode in one of two ways. Either they rode in a loose scatter, fast, well forward onto the withers, whooping it up like they were running buffalo or making war, or they rode far back, almost onto the rump, ambling and limp as half-filled sacks of grain. As far as Stanton had ever been able to tell, the choice of style seemed to be primarily a matter of mood and was subject to instant and incomprehensible change.

Yankees characteristically rode a firm, hard seat with very little ventilation, long in the stirrup and short on the rein, sitting very straight, so as to be almost standing. On the long pull they rode steadily but seldom hard, usually credited as consideration for their mounts, but Stanton suspected it was more likely a basic concern for their own creature comfort.

The Mexicans, as befitted those who had first brought the fine Barbs and Arabs of the original Spanish strains into this country, rode with shorter stirrups and a very loose seat, free-reining and shifting weight with the movements of their mounts so that they actually seemed to be helping their horses along in a rare kind of teamwork. Stanton thought that there must be something to this impression. Certainly they rode the fastest, often for remarkable distances, without undue strain on their horses and for his money they were the most beautiful in saddle.

The approaching riders were Mexican *vaqueros* and he recognized their leader at once. His name was Abelardo. He was Don Felipe Peralta's *segundo* and they called him the wolf of Mora. Not without reason. Although somewhat younger than Stanton, he was a dour and fierce man who only lived for Don Felipe and his interests. Father Frederico, the priest from Taos, often complained that Abelardo did not even trust God when He came to Mora. A mutual respect existed between the Mora *segundo* and Stanton, but it had been hard won.

Stanton remained squatting on his heels as the Mora crew came up. Abelardo swung down and joined him. If he was surprised to see Stanton, he did not show it.

"Where'd you night?" he demanded without greeting or preamble.

"Taylor Springs," Stanton told him. "Part of it, anyway."

"See anything of three men — three thieving *yanquis?*"

Stanton shook his head.

"Too dark. But I shot one of the bastards. Nailed him hard, I think."

"*Bueno!* They jump you?"

"Tried. But I woke up about one minute too soon."

"You're lucky. They'd have killed you for what you have on you and thought nothing of it."

"Like I say, they tried. Why you tailing them, 'Lardo?"

"*Bastardos* is right!" the *segundo* snorted. "They came in to Mora three days ago. Out of the malpais. Said they had some furs and spare gear they wanted to trade for hard money at the ranch store. As you know, that store is not for *yanquis*. Only for our own people. I ran them off. There were some hard words over that."

Stanton smiled. He had seen Abelardo at work with unwanted strangers before.

"I imagine," he said.

63

"I should have followed them," Abelardo growled. "They picked up some of our best beeves. I'm not sure how many. There's a big freight wagon train down past The Meadows, heading in to Santa Fe. The freighters were meat-hungry after the crossing and they sold the beeves to them. Unloaded the other stuff they had to a trader and headed north. When we caught up with the wagons yesterday the beef was butchered, the hides gone, and nothing left for proof."

"I've been wondering when that would start," Stanton said.

"I know when it's going to stop!" Abelardo snapped. "Think they may still be around the springs?"

"Pretty near have to be. They ran last night, but they couldn't go far. Not with a wounded man and no water. My guess is they doubled back as soon as they were sure I'd cleared out —" Stanton hesitated. "Want me to go back with you? I was heading for Santa Fe, but another day or two —"

One of the *segundo's* rare smiles flashed.

"Now you think like a *yanqui, señor.* You think Abelardo and his little ones are not enough. No, *grácias.* This is Mora's business. Mora will attend to it. Will you see Don Felipe on your return?"

"I planned on it."

"Good. I'll tell you then how this business went."

Abelardo rose and called to one of the *vaqueros*.

"Paco, venga aquí, por favór —"

The man rode over and handed down a fine old Hawken muzzle-loader and a beautifully scraped and polished powderhorn. Abelardo handed them to Stanton.

"I bought these from the trader they dealt with on the wagons," he said. "I thought you would want to have them."

Stanton nodded.

"I know. Eli Ferguson. We buried him last week. On the trail at the foot of The Reef. Thanks, 'Lardo. But they're not the ones who killed him. We can't hold them to account for that."

"You're sure?"

Stanton nodded again. Abelardo shrugged and crossed to his horse. As he swung up and started to rein away, Stanton called him.

" 'Lardo — in case you want to put up headstones, their name is Cagle. Three brothers. Matt, Zeke, and Lew Cagle."

CHAPTER SIX

The morning after Spencer Stanton left for Santa Fe, Jaime breakfasted with the Archuletas in the dark in order to make an early start. When 'Mana emerged from her room, Amelio was already in the kitchen and told her that Jaime had gone out to the quarry with Benny and Ramón to resume cutting stone.

She knew, then, that in spite of her protest, Spence had quietly left orders for what was to be done in his absence. She smiled to herself. He was a man of great singleness of purpose. What he said he would build here, he would build. One day the whole structure of the Corona, the whole structure of their lives, would rest solidly on that one fact.

Although it had been altogether her doing, this time, she had no satisfaction from it. It worried her to have him absent from her. Only twenty-four hours and already she felt the aloneness. There was a great sureness in all things in him, a great strength. Only in his absence did she realize how much she fed upon it. This baby they had made in the frequent stormings of their passion would have it, too. This son would be his mirror.

She moved to the room which had been Jaime's. The furnishings were the same, the curtains and the rugs on the flagged floor, but it was strange how soon Jaime's presence was gone from it. The exhausted girl in the bed already dominated it. It was a potent feminine aura which 'Mana could sense. She had never before had another but her own in this house and it was a strange feeling, vaguely disturbing. She smiled again and dismissed it as a part of the heightening of all preceptions which came with the onset of gestation.

The girl still slept soundly. The coverlet was not even disturbed. But the medicinal air was heavy. 'Mana crossed silently and soundlessly opened a window to the bright morning. Going back to the kitchen, she sent Amelio out to invent yard chores so as to avoid having him clattering about within. She shook down the fire and refueled it and set about making a breakfast that would fill the sleeping girl's pitifully flattened belly and take away the taste of her most recent memories.

In a little while she heard Amelio in the yard and warned him around to the back of the house for greater quiet. It was some time after that, she did not know how long, that she heard the horse come into the yard. It was not hard-ridden but there was urgency in the sound. The rider was already down and striding for the door when she opened it. He was not a man she had ever seen before, but she recognized him instantly. A big, well-molded *yanqui* with the dust of long travel heavy on him and the flecks of trouble in his eyes. Spence and Jaime had done well with their descriptions.

'Mana glanced fearfully across the big room to the door beyond which the girl slept and stepped quickly out into the yard. As the man reached her, Amelio came hobbling curiously around the corner of the house with a chopping hoe in his hand. The man's gun leaped out. 'Mana feared he would fire, but he merely gestured peremptorily at Amelio with the weapon. The old man dropped his hoe and approached warily. The big *yanqui* thrust them both into the house ahead of him.

His nose wrinkled appreciatively at the warm odors of the food on the stove and the biscuits in the oven, but his eyes darted cautiously about the room. They came to rest on the door of the room occupied by the sleeping girl.

"Anybody else here?" he asked sharply.

'Mana cringed within but her chin came up.

"At this hour? This is a working ranch."

"Can you doctor, missus?"

"Some."

"A saddlemate with a bullet in him. It's got to come out. Me and my other partner tried, but neither one's got any knack for it and like to killed him. He can't stand much more of that. Can you do better?"

'Mana glanced again at the girl's door, fearful

68

the man's heavy, urgent voice would rouse her and she would show herself. There was no way to warn her that this was her brother — one of those who had killed a man and left her to die in the malpais. As deeply as she had been sleeping, she was not apt to recognize the voice alone in time. Swiftly, 'Mana made up her mind.

"I can try. I'll need some things."

"Get them together," the man said. And to Amelio, "Bring the missus a horse. Keep your mouth shut and don't fetch no trouble back with you. I ain't a forgiving man. You just remember that, old man."

Amelio looked uncertainly at 'Mana, troubled and worried. She nodded, trying to dissuade him from making some foolish attempt by the calmness of her manner. The important thing was to get this man away from the house as quickly as possible.

"Do as he says, Amelio. His — his friend needs help. The *patrón* would want us to do what we can. I'll be perfectly all right."

Reassured, Amelio hobbled out. 'Mana went to a chest for bandaging and scissors. She wanted the stone jar of Ute ointment, but she had left it in Helga's room and could not risk retrieving it. She had to settle for some patent *yanqui* salve in which she had little faith.

When she crossed back to the kitchen area to choose and whet the thinnest boning knife she had, Helga's brother had helped himself to a handful of biscuits from the oven and was bolt-

69

ing them down with thin strips of air-dried venison jerky she was softening and browning in butter in a skillet. She set out the rest of the biscuit tin for him and closed the dampers of the stove. He looked appreciatively about the room again and grinned.

"You live good, missus."

"We work hard."

"*Patrón* — that means boss, don't it?"

'Mana nodded, putting the things she had collected in a clean sugar sack.

"Where is he? Where's your man?"

'Mana could see no point in lying.

"Away. Santa Fe. But our foreman and some of the crew are out at the quarry, if you think we'll need them."

"I seen them. But they didn't me, if that's what you're thinking. Leave be. You and me'll do just fine."

'Mana didn't like his tone or the light in his eyes, but anything to get him out of the house. She tied a knot in the neck of the sugar sack.

"We'd better hurry."

She went out into the yard. He followed, his mouth and hands full of biscuits and jerky. Amelio led up her saddle horse. No one else came up with him, so she knew Raul Archuleta was off somewhere with the stock and only his wife and younger children were down at the adobes. She tied the sack to her saddle and stepped up. She looked down at Amelio and indicated the house.

"Deténgase aquí," she said calmly. *"No permite él que verla."*

With relief she saw that the old man understood at once. He hobbled toward the doorway. He would keep the girl out of sight until they were away, in case she should awaken.

Helga's brother scowled at the swift Spanish phrases.

"That's enough of that, missus. Let's go."

They rode out of the yard. Once away from the house, 'Mana hoped they would meet Jaime or one of the boys coming in with a load of stone, or that they at least would be seen, but all three were out of sight in the arroyo where the quarry lay. She could hear the sound of their hammers ringing distantly across the grass.

In a quarter of a mile a rise of ground cut the location of the quarry off from view.

The brothers' makeshift camp was in a greasewood thicket beside a tiny trickle which drained a small saline slough. 'Mana thought it was about five miles northeast of the Corona headquarters. Far enough for neither smoke nor fire-glow to be visible from the house.

The wounded man, clearly the youngest of the three, lay on a thin pad of hastily plucked rank salt-grass which had been covered by a blanket. His other brother, sitting nearby, rose lazily to his feet and came to them as 'Mana and the one who had brought her rode up. His eyes were frankly, insolently admiring and he reached up

71

for her as she dismounted. His grip remained when her feet touched the ground, hands sliding with easy assurance from under her arms to her breasts, forcing her back against the horse.

"By God, Matt," he said with a grin up at the mounted man, "you do do yourself up first-rate for an old man, don't you? No wonder it took so long. How many times did you stop?"

The one called Matt laughed and swung down.

"We made the best time we could, but I got to admit I did do some thinking."

"Yeah," the other agreed with a chortle. "A man can't hardly help himself, can he?"

'Mana thrust violently, furiously, at him again as he fingered for her nipples.

"God damn you bastards," the wounded man on the ground protested angrily in a thin, rasping voice, "put your peckers back in your pants. Let her at me if she thinks there's anything she can do. That's what she's here for."

"Mighty dangerous to let something like this near a boy as bad off as you," the man molesting 'Mana said. "I bet she could bust your back if you was in first-class shape."

He let his hands drop and stepped back, laughing at 'Mana's fury. She took her sack of needings from her saddle and knelt beside the man on the ground. He was pale about his lips and under his deep tan, but there was a spot of deep flush on the crown of each cheekbone and his eyes were hazed with fever. She thought he had lost a lot of blood and she realized the one called Matt had not summoned help any too soon.

The wound was in the groin, from the front, at the deepest part of the thigh. 'Mana could not be sure, but she thought it was just low enough to have escaped tearing into the belly cavity. She knew that had it done so, retrieval of the bullet would be beyond her limited ability.

The surface of the wound had been considerably lacerated and enlarged, obviously from probing with a beltknife or some other much too large and unwieldy an instrument. It was oozing slowly. Her lips compressed in fresh anger at the callous clumsiness of the other two in inflicting this extra and useless injury. The bullet had to have passed dangerously close to the great artery of the leg and the risk in such unskilled probing had been enormous.

She looked quickly about the camp and realized that she was going to be forced to a more Spartan attempt than she wished. There was no fire, no hot water, no satisfactory utensil to heat it in, and she was none too certain of the alkaline water from the slough, itself. She would have to rely upon the cleanliness of the sugar sack, her own hands and kitchen and storage chest, to lessen the chance of introducing more infection. She straightened on her knees and looked with complete aversion at the other two.

"Hold him," she said tersely. "This leg absolutely must not move."

Matt knelt at his brother's shoulder and spread-eagled out his arms and pinned them down with his weight.

"Think up the best damn cuss words you know, boy," he counseled.

The other brother took his feet, moving obediently when 'Mana gestured sharply with the whetted boning knife that she needed more room. The fact was she could not abide him that near to her. He seemed to realize this in a moment for he reached up and turned back the flap which had been cut in the top of his brother's pants to get at the wound, completely exposing him.

"Let's show the little lady how us Cagle boys is hung," he said. "Might make her a little more friendly."

"Damn your eyes, Zeke," the wounded man exploded furiously. "I wish to hell this was you!"

Matt Cagle reached down and flipped back the flap for decency.

"Get on with it, missus," he growled.

'Mana poised her knife and with an earnest silent prayer slowly lowered its tip into the wound. The body beneath her hands trembled but the leg did not move and there was no outcry. Nearly two thirds of the blade had disappeared before she felt it strike something hard. Hoping desperately that it wasn't bone, she carefully slipped the tip of the knife slightly past it. Lew Cagle's body suddenly went limp. Glancing up quickly, she saw that he had fainted. She did not look at the others.

Holding the knife immobile, she took her scissors and slid them in beside it, using the blade for a guide. Steel slid along steel. When the points of the scissors struck the hard object, she gently expanded them to make a pincers of the points. On the second try she felt them grip, however precariously. Slowly, ever so carefully, she withdrew the two implements from the wound together.

When they were clear and she relaxed her grip, a small, round, heavy object fell from between the scissors points into her lap.

"I'll be goddamned!" Matt Cagle said, not without some awe.

'Mana grabbed up one of the towels she had brought in her sack and lurched to her feet and ran to the little creek. Kneeling unsteadily there, she washed in its bitter saline water, sloshing her face as well and fighting to control her churning nausea.

Suddenly she felt herself seized from behind and pulled over backward into the grass on her back. Then Zeke Cagle was half atop her, pinning her down with his odorous body, one arm pinioning both of hers. The bristles of his beard scraped her. His mouth, wide and hot and wet, clamped voraciously over hers. She struggled frantically, trying to dislodge his crushing weight. His free hand grabbed at the hem of her skirt and jerked it to her waist.

Screaming within in fury and outrage and a more horrible fear than she had ever known, choking and suffocating, she writhed and twisted with all of the desperate strength of her body.

There was no sound but the man's stertorous breathing. Then, suddenly, one word cracked out like a pistol shot.

"Zeke!"

Cagle lifted his head and froze. 'Mana turned hers and could see the other two brothers. Matt was squatting calmly on his heels, a small half-smile on his lips, no more than an interested spectator. Lew, her patient, had regained consciousness. He was sitting half up, paler than before, resting on one elbow. His other hand held a cocked pistol leveled across the updrawn knee of his uninjured leg at his brother.

"Get off," he ordered tautly. "Let her up."

"Oh, hell, Lew," the man pinioning 'Mana protested. "She's took care of you. Now's my turn."

"So help me, I'll blow your goddamned head off," the wounded man warned.

Matt turned his head without otherwise moving.

"I think he means it, Zeke."

Zeke grunted, freed 'Mana, and clumsily got to his feet, staring lewdly down at her as she hastily pulled down her skirt and sat up, sucking for breath.

"Damn it, she's had plenty afore now," the man grumbled. "A little more won't hurt."

Matt rose, tilted his head at Zeke in signal, and moved off. Zeke followed. They stopped out of earshot and stood there talking. Lew let down the hammer on his pistol and eased back on his

76

blanket. Trying to compose herself with something for her hands to do, 'Mana found her towel
and damped it and went back to him.

She washed his leg about the wound as best
she could without further contaminating it and
packed it with the *yanqui* salve and bound it
tightly to give pressure support and keep out as
much dirt as possible. The wounded man
watched her silently as she worked. When she
was finished and was gathering her things back
into the sugar sack, he spoke.

"Feels a hell of a lot better," he said with a
deep breath. He paused a moment. "I'm sorry,
ma'am. He's a son of a bitch. We all are."

Composure returned, 'Mana nodded. She
suddenly wanted to hear the sound of her own
voice to see if the scream was actually gone.

"Who shot you?"

The wounded man's face twisted wryly.

"A loner we was aiming to jump for his kit and
poke," he said. "A little more loot for a long ride.
Ain't that the hell of it?"

He sucked at a breath.

"We was past your place a spell back. Matt figured it was the only spot we could try hereabouts
for help. This was as far as I could get, the shape
I was in."

He paused again and gingerly moved the injured leg.

"Thanks," he said. "You done a good job."

'Mana rose and went to her horse and was
retieing the sugar sack to her saddle when Matt

returned to her. She saw that Zeke was squatting beside his wounded brother.

"How long'll it be before he can ride, if we took it real easy?"

'Mana shrugged.

"Only a few days, with luck, I think" — she glanced back at the miserable camp — "if he had half a chance."

"Which he sure ain't got here."

"You'll have to find a cleaner spot, with better air and water."

"Cleanest spot I know of hereabouts is that house of yours."

'Mana shivered involuntarily but controlled the fear and aversion and stiffened proudly.

"I promise you that if Spencer Stanton ever sets eyes on any of you —"

"He won't," Matt Cagle cut in easily. "Santa Fe's a long way, round trip. Eats up a lot of time. A few days, you said. Lew'll be fit again and we'll be long gone for the River when he gets back."

"Our foreman and crew —"

Cagle interrupted her with a confident smile.

"When the boss is away you give the orders, don't you, missus? Or can. It'll be just like it was with the old man this morning. Neighborly. Common decency. Poor, unfortunate boy, way-laid on the Trail. Can't leave him out here to die. You can make it stick. 'Cause you're going to have to."

'Mana was not misled by the man's easy manner. She knew exactly what he was saying. She

78

had the full measure of these men, now. She knew the merciless, calculated brutality of which they were capable. She remembered Helga and thought swiftly.

"It's miles to the ranch," she said. "Your brother couldn't sit a saddle nearly that far, now. If he starts to bleed again before a good clot is formed, he'll be finished in a few minutes, and not a thing in the world anyone can do."

"Don't you worry your pretty little head about that," Matt Cagle said. "The best ain't none too good for Lew. We'll fetch him along just as easy and comfortable as he's lying there right now."

He reached up and jerked the sugar sack loose from her saddle.

"I'll just take this along. That's a mighty sharp knife you've got in here. Come along nice, now, and sit a spell while we break camp."

He took her elbow. She jerked her arm free but went with him back to the wounded man's pad because, as he said, she had to.

In a few minutes Matt and Zeke Cagle got their other horses saddled and their gear up. They cut a big, cot-sized bundle of the longest greasewood stalks and tied their butt ends securely together with a saddle rope. Two more ropes were made fast for towing.

They picked up their brother, blanket and all, and stretched him atop the bound brush as on a featherbed. He seemed reasonably comfortable and 'Mana realized that the tough, resilient greasewood fibers would cushion him from most obstacles and would drag easily across the grass if they stayed on turf.

When they were ready, she was told to mount up. Zeke Cagle took one of the two tow ropes and dallied it about his saddle horn. Matt brought the other to 'Mana and made it fast to her saddle.

"Just so you don't get a notion to bolt off when our hands is full," he said.

"Why didn't you bring him in like this this morning in the first place?" she asked.

"Because we didn't know you'd be so neighborly and your man so obliging as to be gone," he answered. "Now, missus, you get one thing straight. You make any mistake when we get there, I'll personally see to it that Zeke gets his crack at you without Lew or anyone else around to make him climb off until he's through and has had all he wants. That can take a long time with Zeke."

He slapped the rump of her horse. Zeke Cagle started up at the same time. Slack came out and the brush sled began to move.

CHAPTER SEVEN

Jaime came back to the house with the Archuleta boys and a load of stone at noon. He wasn't at first too disturbed by Amelio's report of the reason for 'Mana Stanton's absence. She had lived long on this land and knew it better than any of them. Father Frederico had some Spanish books on medicine at Taos. He taught her much out of them when he was tutoring her, even when she was still a girl. So had her friends, the Utes.

She had a way with illness and injury, as he had discovered from personal experience. He knew it was a private prejudice, but he doubted there was a professional doctor in New Mexico her equal. And she was too compassionate to refuse any reasonable plea for help.

But it did trouble him that there were more strangers on Corona grass. 'Mana's words about them troubled him as well. He hoped Spencer Stanton would return with some kind of an answer to this growing problem. And he felt obliged to scold Amelio, if only on general principles.

"Damn it, you could have gone with her, you know," he said as they came into the house from the yard. "I know you can't work a saddle, but you can still sit one if all you have to do is hang on. Why didn't you saddle up, too?"

The old man pointed across the room. Jaime turned. The girl from the malpais stood in the open doorway of his old room. She had found a clean dress of 'Mana's. An old one she frequently wore to work about the house. A pair of worn moccasins were on the girl's feet. Her hair, washed and brushed out to a high sheen, hung in a heavy, golden blond cascade down her back, a striking contrast to the deep violet of her eyes. She was pale and thin but Jaime saw what he had not noted before. She had long, slender legs, hinted in outline beneath the dress, well rounded hips, and her high, outthrusting breasts were full and firm.

He liked it all and his smile betrayed him. She smiled back, then sobered, her eyes smoky as the smile died in them. She came on into the room to them, stepping gingerly with her sore feet. Jaime instinctively stepped forward to take her arm. Her flesh was warm and firm to his touch. He was self-consciously surprised that he should note it. Her arm seemed to clamp his fingers lightly against her side in response. He led her to one of the big chairs. She sank gratefully into it.

"My dogs ain't quite up to snuff this morning," she said apologetically.

Her rank, nasal, river-bottom dialect had a familiar sound to Jaime's Missouri-honed ears, discordant in comparison with the liquid, cadenced Spanish of the land and Spencer Stanton's educated, well-spoken Virginia English which were the tongues of the Corona. But her voice was low, throaty, and warm in spite of this handicap. A woman's voice. Like 'Mana's.

"How you feel?" he asked solicitously.

"Middling, otherwise. I should, after all she done for me. That bed and the whopping bait of grub the old man cooked up for me this morning and all. He's right. About her being gone. It's all account of me."

"*La patrona* told me to stay with the *señorita* in case she woke up," Amelio, explained anxiously. "She said she would be all right. She said the *patrón* would want it that way."

He paused, blinking his own puzzlement.

"Then, when they were already in saddle — in Spanish, so he wouldn't understand, I think — she told me to keep the *señorita* from being seen by this man as they rode away."

Jaime looked sharply back to the girl.

"The mister told you about them — who they are — what happened out there?" she asked.

Jaime nodded. She looked up at him with troubled eyes.

"It's them, all right. I feel it in my bones. It's got to be. Rotten scum! Somehow, she knew, too. The one that come here — Matt, I think, from what he told me —" She indicated Amelio. "She went with him to keep him from finding out I was here and finishing up what they tried to finish out there in the lava. Mister, I'm scared for her!"

83

Jaime nodded again. He was, himself. More than he cared to admit. And for this girl, as well. He found himself realizing that he could not abide the thought of that lovely, long-limbed body subjected to abuse again.

"Can you ride — maybe only an hour or two — into the mountains?" he asked her.

"To hell and back, if there's need," she agreed.

"There's need," he assured her flatly. "Afraid of Indians?"

"I ain't afraid of nothing that's friendly and decent. Unless it's too damned friendly."

"Good," Jaime said. He turned to Amelio. "There's need for you, too, old man," he said. "Listen good. I'm going out on the grass and find the *patrona*. I don't know what the hell I'll run into. Not with these *cabrones*. There may not even be a wounded man out there. The one that come after her may just have told her that to get her to come with him."

"You know them a damned sight better than I thought," the girl told him.

"Saddle two horses, good ones," he continued to Amelio. "While you're at the corrals, tell Ramón and Benny to get back to the quarry as soon as they've eaten and work there all afternoon unless they hear from me. If their father comes in from the range, ask Mama Archuleta to send him out to join the boys and to keep everybody else down there away from the house. The *patrona* may come back alone, but one or more of them may come back with her, depending on what their real wants are, and I might miss them out there.

"The one that come for the *patrona* must have seen the boys and me at the quarry this morning. Or heard us, sure. And he knows what the setup here at the house was when they left. If some of them do come back with her and there's nobody at the quarry or things look different here, they might get suspicious of a trap and do something to harm her. *Comprende, amigo?*"

Amelio's head bobbed earnestly.

"Get the *señorita* out of here just as soon as you can," Jaime went on. "Take her to Chato. With luck the Utes will be in their lower camp, but find them. Leave her with Chato's mother. Bring him back with you. As many of his friends as he can lay hand to in a hurry. Have him hide their horses somewhere west of the house, where they can't be stumbled onto. Plant his men as close to the house as he can without them being seen.

"Warn him that no matter what happens, not to make a move till I show up. I know men like these better than he does and I don't want any chance of a mistake that might get the *patrona* hurt."

"*Sí,* Jaime, *entiédolo todo,*" Amelio said.

He hobbled to the door. Jaime momentarily stopped him there.

"*Amigo,* when you get back, take your place in the house like everything's just as it was when she left. Even if there's some kind of a hard time, don't you do anything foolish. If I'm not with her and they are, wait for me."

Jaime paused, then resumed, his voice hardening.

"Get back here as soon as you can. If I miss her and some of them come, too, there's a chance they might get here before you. I don't want that to happen if we can keep from it. Every minute the *patrona*'s with bastards like these, the more danger she's in."

The old man crossed himself and went out the door, hurrying toward the corrals.

Jaime took his rifle and belt, and the Spanish pistol Governor Armijo had given him long ago as a boy, from the racks over the fireplace. As he armed himself, he tried to reassure the girl from the malpais.

"You'll be safe with the Utes. You're from this house. They'll treat you real dandy, at least in their way. As quick as 'Mana's back and we're dead sure your brothers have cleared the country with no chance of coming back, we'll send for you. And don't worry too much about her. When it comes to taking care of herself, she's a better man than most I've known."

"A better woman, too," the girl said quietly. "You find her, mister. You bring her back."

Jaime pulled his belt tight and went out to his waiting horse. He had on occasion faced heavy responsibility since Spencer Stanton had rescued him from involuntary servitude to an unprincipled bully in a freight-wagon string, but a heavy foreboding was in him. He feared that none had been as grave as this.

His horse was fresh from grazing all morning while he worked in the quarry with the Archuleta boys. Jaime was grateful for that accident of event.

He had a choice as he left the Corona yard and he made it without hesitation. 'Mana and her escort had left tracks. That was inescapable. But it almost immediately became evident that the man's intent was to leave as few as possible. Directly trailing them would be tedious and time-consuming work, and time was the important consideration.

At half a mile he looked back and saw with satisfaction that Amelio and the girl from the malpais were already mounted and lining west for the mountains at a run. He kicked his own mount up and rode hard due east for the course of Conejo Creek. He reasoned that the girl's brothers had camped there before and, knowing wood was available and the water sweet, had probably holed up somewhere along the creek again.

Walking his horse occasionally to blow before resuming a steady lope, he made good time. Just short of two hours, he rode down into the Conejo draw. There were no fresh tracks on either bank. Here he made his second choice, a blind one, and turned north up the stream toward the great, looming barrier of The Reef.

Luck was with him. In twenty minutes he hit the fresh tracks of three horses. They came in from the east in the direction of the Trail at Taylor Springs or thereabouts and crossed Conejo Creek without even a pause to water. On the far bank they lined out parallel to a small alkaline trickle in practically a bee line for the Corona headquarters.

That they had not watered betrayed urgency, and when he crossed, Jaime found the reason. On a rock at water's edge were a few drops of blood which were yet viscous to the touch. It was possible that 'Mana had gone on what she believed to be a legitimate errand of mercy.

Four or five miles further on he found their deserted campsite and the grass pad beside which 'Mana had made her ministrations. He saw the cut mesquite stalks at the edge of the thicket and thereafter the trail was easy to follow. The brush ambulance drag they towed left a wide mark and there were the tracks of five horses which he read as 'Mana's, those of the three brothers, and a pack animal.

He would have felt relief to the point of believing the precautions he had taken at the ranch house unnecessary, but for one thing. Under ordinary circumstances, it would be 'Mana Stanton's nature to bring an injured man in where he could be given better care if it was safe to move him. He supposed the brothers were relying on this. But she would not bring these three in if they all were dying. Not when she thought their sister was at the house and certain to be discovered. So she was doing so under some kind of duress.

He could already hear the hammers of Raul Archuleta and his boys at the quarry when he unexpectedly came upon 'Mana's cavalcade in a little swale which concealed them to the last moment, almost within sight of the Corona house. The lashings on their brush ambulance drag had apparently loosened and it had started to disintegrate. They had stopped to make repairs and were just starting up again when he hit the rim of the swale and was onto them without warning.

The wounded man on the drag seemed comfortable enough. One of the two ropes was fast to 'Mana's saddle. One of the brothers had the other. The third was leading a pack horse and a riderless saddle animal bloodied to the ground on the right side, horn to hocks.

'Mana, looking back, saw him first. He could sense her relief in the cant of her body. However, she waved to him as she would under untroubled circumstances, with no visible sign of distress. She spoke to the men and pulled up, halting the caravan again.

The brothers watched his approach without any particular outward wariness. It was only when he was very close that Jaime saw that the oldest — the one who had been spokesman when he and Spencer Stanton had first seen them — had a cocked pistol across his lap, bearing on

'Mana at almost point-blank range. He grinned when he saw Jaime's reaction.

"I see you remember us and I remember you, bucko-boy," he said. "Now just you be almighty careful or the missus'll get herself hurt some."

Jaime cursed himself for getting caught so flat-footed.

"Do whatever he says, Jaime," 'Mana cut in quickly. "That's an order. It's all right. Everything's all right."

"Except them guns," the man with the pistol said. "They make me nervous. Get 'em, Zeke."

The man on the other tow rope dismounted and approached Jaime warily. Jaime realized there was nothing he could do without endangering 'Mana. He reluctantly surrendered his belt gun and rifle. The man in the saddle holstered his pistol with satisfaction.

"Better," he said. "Don't aim to crowd you none, but you wasn't none too friendly, last time we met, and when you already got one brother shot, you get kind of careful-like."

"What's this supposed to mean?" Jaime demanded angrily. His sharp gesture included the group. The spokesman smiled mockingly.

"Hankering for a little of your greaser hospitality."

"God damn you, I told you once before, we don't use that word on this ranch!"

The man glanced at 'Mana and smirked.

"So you did. I clean forgot. We aim to put up with you till Lew, there, can sit saddle again.

90

The missus invited."

'Mana nodded, obviously against her will.

"I got the bullet out of him, but he wouldn't have stood a chance in the camp they had. He'll do better where I can take care of him for a few days. That's all, Jaime. Just a few days. We can make do."

"Spence wouldn't stand for it," Jaime protested. "Not a damned minute!"

"He isn't here, and they know it."

"Then I won't. Not by a damn sight!"

"I'll give the orders," 'Mana said firmly. "You go on ahead and tell them everything's all right. Have them start getting things ready down at the adobes."

It was the first time 'Mana had pulled rank on him in more than five years, but Jaime realized she had cause. She was thinking of these men's sister. He wanted to reassure her that there was no concern on that score, but there was no way. He admired her calm and shrewdness. He thought that if he could get far enough ahead, he could cut around unseen to the quarry. Benny and Ramón Archuleta would have armed themselves before going back out, after Amelio's warning. If their father was with them, too, the Corona might give these rough-handed bastards a warmer welcome than they could use.

"If that's the way you want it, *patrona*," he said meekly.

He started to lift his reins. The man with the pistol touched it and shook his head.

"Now you know he ain't going to do any such damn thing, missus," he said chidingly. "He's going to be real gentlemanly. He's going to take over that tow for you so you can ride right along close to me and we're all going on in together, nice and friendly-like, so we get a nice, friendly-like welcome."

Jaime saw the glimmer of hope die in 'Mana's eyes. He reined over and transferred the tow rope from the horn of her saddle to his own. The spokesman nodded approval and rode up tight beside 'Mana and they started moving again.

As he rode, Jaime recalculated time and distance for the hundredth time. It looked like there wasn't going to be any practical way to reach or alert the Archuletas and he was afraid that there was no possibility that Amelio and the girl could have reached even the lower of the Ute camps soon enough for the old man and the Utes to have gotten back and set up an ambush. So his plans would not work.

He was going to have to watch Spence Stanton's pregnant wife be herded back to her own house with the situation fully in the control of these worthless animals. And once they were forted up on the ranch with her as hostage, even the Utes would be powerless to dislodge them. The risk would be too great.

Nevertheless, as they directly approached the yard, he found himself watching eagerly for some sign Chato and his men were in place after all, waiting for his signal. Chato would have left some mark to tell him they were ready. But he could discover none.

'Mana pulled up in the dooryard and pointed off toward the corrals.

"We have a couple of comfortable little houses down there," she said authoritatively. "You and your brothers can have one of them. Jaime will show you."

"Unh-uh, missus," the spokesman said. "No hired hand's shack for me. I said your house and your house it is. Right here. I fancy that good living I seen. All three of us." He swung down easily. "Zeke, you and the bucko-boy fetch along Lew. Me and the missus'll go pick our rooms for us."

Zeke swung down and started back toward the drag on which his wounded brother lay. The spokesman moved to her stirrup and reached up to give 'Mana a lift down. She surprised the hell out of her horse by swinging her near leg high over the horn of her saddle and vaulting down on the off side.

The startled animal wheeled away from such an unorthodox dismount, solidly jostling the man waiting beside the empty near stirrup. Jaime sensed instantly what she was attempting. As 'Mana quit saddle, so did he, intending to create as much additional diversion for her as he could.

'Mana landed with skirts kilted high, running desperately for the door of the house, behind which was a stout bar, ready to drop, and weap-

93

ons, always kept loaded, to which she could lay hand. She flashed past Jaime as he lunged in the opposite direction around her dancing, snorting horse.

The startled spokesman had regained his balance and was reaching for his pistol. Jaime hit him cleanly with a short, powerful Missouri chop which had all of his frustration and anger and outraged resentment behind it. By its sound and jolt the blow should have felled an ox. The man slackened but somehow retained his feet, shaking his head, dazed only momentarily. Jaime eagerly jerked him around to finish him off, but an anguished scream sounded behind him.

"Jaime!"

He thrust the man stumblingly from him and wheeled. The one called Zeke had intercepted 'Mana at the door, just as she tripped the latch. The door had swung open, but Zeke was dragging her away from it, back across the veranda. In the frenzy of her struggle, her dress had been ripped from one shoulder.

In three pumping strides, Jaime charged into Zeke at full speed, carrying all three of them back across the veranda. The doorsill cut their feet from under them and they went down in a hard, abrasive sprawl on the flagstone flooring within. As they went down, the spokesman's pistol fired in the yard. The ball passed through the doorway somewhere above them and ricocheted from the stone of the far wall.

Jaime jerked Zeke's head back by his hair and ground knuckles into his eye sockets. The man roared and Jaime rolled him over his own body to free 'Mana and saw the spokesman loom in the doorway, hurtling through it with his discharged pistol reversed in his hand and upraised like a hammer. He braced himself for the blow, but it didn't come.

One of the heavy chairs came sailing across the room, smashing into the man with the pistol as one had recently smashed into Spencer Stanton. And old Amelio was right behind it, leaping astride the man as he went down. Suddenly legs were about, everywhere, pouring from the bedroom at each end of the big main room. Moccasin-shod and buckskin-clad legs. Hard hands were roughly subduing Zeke, jerking him up from Jaime and flattening him against the stone of the walls. It had taken less than ten seconds in all.

A gentler hand offered Jaime an assist and when he was back on his feet he found himself facing the handsome, powerful figure of Chato, the Ute.

"*Como está?*" the Indian asked anxiously.

"*Bién, ahora,*" Jaime said. "*Grácias,* old friend."

He glanced around. There were more than a dozen Indians in the room. Amelio had abandoned the felled spokesman to some of them and they were dragging him unceremoniously to his feet. The old man was solicitously wrapping a jacket about 'Mana's scratched shoulders to

95

cover her torn dress. He looked back to Chato.

"We were hunting pronghorns at the mouth of the canyon when Amelio and the girl came," the Ute said. "So there was time. I sent the *señorita* on to my camp with two to guard her and show her the way and we came on here."

He grinned at Jaime.

"To hide the horses was easy," he continued. "In the arroyo half a mile west. But to make an ambush close enough to this house to do any good, that is impossible, *compadre*. Even for Mountain Utes. You and *señor* Stanton saw to that long ago. So why not the house, the bedrooms? These *cabrones* would never expect that."

Chato was obviously pleased with the simplicity of his stratagem. Jaime nodded, still shaken, but with his anger reheating as he glared at the two held helpless against the wall by Chato's men. He crossed to 'Mana.

"Are you all right, *mamasita?*" he asked gently.

She nodded, rapidly regaining her composure.

"Are you sure you — you feel all right?"

In his attempt at delicacy he inadvertently let his eyes drop to her figure.

"A woman is more indestructible than you think, Jaime," she said. "So is a baby, at this stage of the game. If that's what you mean."

He flushed but went on insistently.

"Did they mistreat you, out there?"

"Let's not talk about it."

"Damn it, I want to know. So will Spence."

96

"Why don't you let him ask me, then?"

"So help me, 'Mana, if they so much as looked cross-eyed at you —"

She wearily brushed a stray lock of hair back from her eyes.

"Please, Jaime, if you don't mind. I've had enough for one day. It's over. Forget it, now. There are more important things."

"The *patrona*'s right, *amigo*," Chato interceded, "Like what to do with this pair and that wounded one outside. Got any ideas?"

Jaime turned and recrossed to the two brothers against the wall. He planted himself solidly before them.

"You bet hell I do," he said grimly. "I've got a couple of real dandies."

CHAPTER EIGHT

Stanton nighted again and breakfasted in the half-light of false dawn. He enjoyed the awakening, invigorating air and the peaceful solitude of the hour. In this borning time, the vastness of the high country was scaled down. To the immediate. To the closest shapes and silhouettes. There was great silence. The night was gone; the day not yet arrived.

A man loomed largest to himself, then. He was not dwarfed by what he could not yet see. It was necessary reassurance. Even the strongest could not long survive here unless he could occasionally stand as tall as the mountains, themselves, in the secret eye of his mind.

Stanton was in saddle before the sun burst out of the *llanos estacados*. It was his fourth morning away from the Corona. The Trail had gained all its southing. It swung with the sun directly into the southern ramparts of the Sangre de Cristos. Ahead was the lift to the summit of Glorieta Pass and the short downhill run into Santa Fe. It was a hard pull for the big freight rigs of the trade, but easy and comfortable for an unhurried saddleman.

As the morning warmed, mountain creatures

began to appear. Perky chipmunks, impishly skittering across the track ahead of a traveler instead of prudently waiting in safety and crossing unnoticed behind. A cadre of crested blue jays, raucously protesting intrusion and passing the word ahead like sentinels. Drumming grouse, exploding from trailside and winging away, low and fast, sailing with amazing accuracy through a maze of sapling and thicket. Deer, feeding in a slanted meadow below a stand of silver aspen, stunted and blackened by living too low. Fat marmots, whistling in the high rocks.

Nearing the summit, Stanton overtook the freight string to which the Cagles had sold some stolen Mora cattle. He found the trader to whom they had disposed of the contents of Fergy Ferguson's pack. The one from whom the wolf of Mora had bought the mountain man's rifle and powderhorn as mementos for him. He swung aboard the wagon to examine the pack as they jolted along. He found what he was hoping for in Fergy's possibles bag. A suitable memento of the old man for 'Mana, as well.

It was a sewing kit, encased in a folding, handmade pouch. There were needles, neatly graded by size. The shape of the heads and cut of the eyes were not quite like any he had seen before. All were still so sharp he realized they had been hand-honed to fresh keenness many times in their span of service.

There was a thimble, too small for any man's blunt fingertip, and a device of thick, hardened leather like a sailmaker's palm, fitted to the heel of the hand for forcing a needle through buckskin or other stubborn material. There were hanks of linen thread and lengths of cured sinew and a lump of beeswax and fine, beautifully engraved Sheffield scissors in two sizes.

Like the needles, the scissors were differently made. Stanton realized the steel in the kit must be very old. He was intrigued by the woman's thimble. Its size made its use by the trapper for any practical purpose impossible. Yet no mountain man would retain a useless possession and carry it about with him for years unless he fancied it as a potent personal charm or it had some deep sentimental significance.

With Fergy, it had to be the latter. The thought was inviting. Solitary old Fergy had once loved a woman enough to carry her scissors and needles and thimble with him through the years and into the farthest reaches of the mountains. It was a pleasing fancy. He paid the trader his price and took the kit and transferred from the wagon back to his saddle. He thought 'Mana would be pleased with the gift.

The sun was low when Stanton rode into Santa Fe. The city always pleased him, but this time he was vaguely troubled. A number of new houses and commercial buildings were under construction. Santa Fe had always seemed as timeless as the gray-pink of its adobe walls. A permanence almost as ancient as the earth itself. It had always seemed this changelessness would

100

continue to extend as endlessly into the future as it did into the past.

He had come to accept this as did most New Mexicans of his acquaintance, by faith and conviction rather than by logic. He pulled up at a corner where new walls were rising on the old foundations of a ruin which had been destroyed by private disaster or neglect and its original adobe long since melted back into the earth. He asked the two old men who were laying up the new mud bricks for whom they were building the house. They seemed surprised at the question, as though the answer was common knowledge to all.

"For a *yanqui,* of course," one answered. "I have not been told the name."

"Why the 'of course'?"

"What walls are put up in Santa Fe these days but to make room for more of you?"

"Building's your trade. I should think that's good."

"Oh, we can use the work, *señor.* But forgive me if I say it — I could do with less pay and fewer foreigners."

"What's so bad about being a *yanqui, amigo?* We all have to be something."

"*Seguro que si.* To be one *yanqui* is nothing. I speak with you, do I not? But so many — that is different. You can become too many. Then, suddenly, it is not our city anymore. It is not Santa Fe. It is not New Mexico. Maybe not even Mother Mexico, herself. It is some foreign place

101

and we no longer have a home. God forbid that, *señor!*"

The workman shook his head lugubriously, as though the doomsday he foresaw was already upon the land. He returned to his adobe bricks. Sobered, Stanton rode on. He realized more was being altered than the walls of Santa Fe. He was beginning to see how wise 'Mana had been in urging him to come here now. She was right. However faintly, the winds of change were starting to blow. They might presage storm.

For more than two hundred years, Santa Fe had centered about the plaza. The entire north side of this plain, packed-earth square was enclosed by the long, low, veranda-shaded facade of its first major building, the *palacio de los gobernadores*. On the east was the squat, cross-topped bell tower of the Parroquia. On the southeast corner was the tavern of La Fonda, a sprawling adobe inn and stable and wagon yard which was the official terminus of the Santa Fe Trail. The west and south were closed in by a few of the more pretentious residences, some small shops, and the principal trading and business houses of the city.

Stanton put himself and his horse up at La Fonda and returned to the plaza. Opposite the *palacio* was a business establishment much altered since his last visit. The sign over the entry was the same: *"Wetzel y Cia."* But Wetzel & Company had taken over an adjoining front, doubling the size of the store. Since he and 'Mana were participants in the "Company" portion of Wetzel's firm, Stanton was well pleased with the expansion.

Wetzel's white shock of erectile hair, his slight frame, narrow, intelligent features, and brisk business manner were unchanged. He was with a customer. Stanton sauntered the aisles. He had not realized how quickly time had passed and how isolated they were on the Corona. The diversity of merchandise now available to the Santa Fe trade astonished him. He thought Wetzel's stock on hand had increased half again since his last visit.

Presently the trader finished with the customer, called a clerk from a storeroom at the rear to tend to any others, and hurried to Stanton, throwing his arms wide in the spontaneous Spanish *abrazo* of old friends, met again.

"Spence! What's this? I thought it was your working season."

"What's to work, the size herd I've been able to scrape up? It's my suspicious nature. Figured I'd better check your books."

"Ha! You'd never catch me, *amigo*. No dung-booted cow nurse. But 'Mana — how's our lovely 'Mana?"

"Pretty, pregnant, and proud as hell, Sol."

"The devil! A miracle, yet! An old fart like you." He checked himself and solemnly held up his hand. "May it be a man-child," he added, formally and earnestly invoking an ancient rune

103

of his race. "I'll buy a drink to 'Mana."

"Sure, you damned bandit," Stanton accused with a grin, "and charge it to my account behind my back."

They went into a small room off the original store, in which Wetzel yet lived and kept his books. He also still kept whiskey under his cot. They had their drink to 'Mana Stanton's health and condition. Wetzel poured them another.

"I've missed that in life, Spence," he said ruefully. "The helpmate. The seed on fallow ground. God will hold me to account, I suppose."

Stanton laughed at him. The thought of Sol Wetzel as a married man and procreator of a family was too incongruous. Business, the sparring excitement and continuous if usually bloodless warfare of buy and sell, was Wetzel's total life. There was no room for anything else. There never would be.

"Don't take it too hard," he comforted the trader slyly. "It's never too late. Really a pretty simple process, once you get the hang of it."

"Yeah, you tell me," Wetzel snorted. "It's only taken you eight years."

"Seven!" Stanton protested in mock indignation. "Damn it, if you're going to malign my manhood, let's get down to business."

"Music to my ears."

"Pretty important occasion, Sol. And I'm adding to the house. Need a hell of a lot of stuff. Afraid a packstring won't do, this time. I'd like to try a good, stout light wagon, if you can find me one."

"Wetzel can do anything. One wagon and a four-up team for a start. What next?"

"This is sure going to put a dent in my account."

"Maybe not as much as you think. You saw the new floor space, how I've let the inventory build up. That's because I've had to start using your money in the store operation, buying and selling to your account, too."

"Whoa, now!" Stanton protested in surprise. "You're not obliged to do that. Just manage 'Mana's and my share of the raw wool trade."

"That's it. The wool's been turning a good profit. Enough so's I've had to find another place to put your share for you. I can't abide seeing idle money piling up in a strongbox. General merchandise seemed as good for you as it's been for me, so you got a share in that stock out front."

Stanton shook his head firmly. "No go, Sol, That's above and beyond. 'Mana wouldn't approve. Neither do I."

"Forget it," Wetzel said with a grin. "I'm charging you a healthy commission, coming and going. You know me, *amigo*. If I can't make a profit off a friend and partner, he isn't worth having for either. I can't afford that kind of luxury."

"The Midas touch." Stanton smiled with wry amusement.

"Oh, hell, Spence, nobody's perfect. I get my tail in a crack, ever now and then." Wetzel paused and rubbed his chin ruefully. "I don't suppose you got wind of it, but we had us a little ruckus a while back. A bunch from Texas organized themselves into a private expedition and invaded our border, way out yonder, east of you.

"Tried to pretend it was a peaceful demonstration to support the Lone Star Republic's claim against Mexico for everything east of the Rio Grande. Bastards. Trying to move the line better'n two hundred miles west of where it was put by treaty. Including Santa Fe, itself. The Corona, too, for that matter."

Stanton frowned with fresh concern. Here was another facet of what 'Mana had sensed. Texas settlers were becoming more and more ebullient since they had won independence from Mexico. Goliad, San Jacinto, and the Alamo were justification for public as well as private ambition. But he found it difficult to believe that Texas wanted more land, more graze, or could use it. Not with the already vast area it had wrested from Mexico. Most of the new Republic was even more sparsely settled than the high country itself.

He thought it was only a few of the most aggressive and that it was size, alone, which appealed to them. Sheer space and extent. And most of these hated Mexico and all things Mexican. With them, vanity and conquest could be the only motives. Empire-builders, in their way, as he was himself, he supposed.

106

"I don't know about the lot," Wetzel continued, "but some of them sure as hell meant business. They formed some kind of a secret syndicate and gathered up a big bunch of good range cattle. Longhorns, mostly. Lord knows from where. Two thousand head. They drove it right up to the existing line and had it held there, ready to push across in a hurry if their damned 'peaceful invasion' worked."

For the first time, Stanton felt a sharp surge of interest, far more personal than the natural indignation of a New Mexican citizen. From the first season, his compelling need had been cattle. Two thousand head! Enough to be the salvation of the Corona and the means to the making of his dream. He tried to conceal the thought which struck him.

"What happened?" he asked casually.

"The scheme went bust," Wetzel said. "Too many generals, I'd guess. Texicans are like that unless they got a Sam Houston or somebody to knock their ears down. Governor Armijo stopped them cold before they'd crossed over very far. Killed a few and hauled in the rest."

The trader downed his drink without relish and poured another.

"The governor's a slick one. He found out about that herd being held out there on the Staked Plains and saw a way to squeeze a good ransom out of the Texicans. To make himself look good here and in Mexico City. Not on them but on their stock. So he declared the herd confiscated as indemnity for the invasion.

"But the Texicans turned the tables on him. They refused to cough up a cent. Armijo blew up and shipped them all off under arrest to prison in Mexico City. That's where I came in, smart son of a bitch that I am. I know Armijo. I figured he'd make a real good deal to save face. So I made him a private cash offer, which he could publicly announce, in trade for New Mexican title to that herd, where was and as was, at a shameful fraction of its real value on the hoof. He took me up like a shot."

"You got it?" Stanton demanded incredulously. "Damn you, Sol, why didn't you declare 'Mana and me in on that instead of your blasted store?"

"You were already in. And I didn't need you on this. With those Texicans already in the Mexico City prison, where they couldn't protest or likely even get word out, I figured I had a cinch. No owners to claim the cattle or order them moved. I could leave them right where they were and sell them off locally in small lots for whatever I could get. Who'd ask questions if they were getting bargains? I could sure afford to give them that, no skin off my ass at all. Then the lid fell in. The governor got word two days ago."

"Somebody else got their hands on that herd?" Stanton asked, more disappointed than he realized.

"Not yet, but might as well," Wetzel said sourly. "How do you figure? A damned, stupid political accident. You probably know the Lone

108

Star's been trying to make bad blood between Mexico and the States ever since it got its independence. So Austin yelled its blamed head off to Washington over this illegal foreign arrest of its innocent, well-meaning, peaceful citizens. Bullcrap! Innocent and well-meaning when they were miles into Mexican territory when Armijo stopped them!"

"The hell with politics," Stanton said impatiently. "Is that herd still there?"

"Likely. What's the difference, now? Plenty in Congress have been wanting to annex Texas. Probably to keep it from claiming half the States, too. So they want to keep the Texicans friendly. They got Washington to pile some tough pressure on Mexico City. *El presidente* gave in and turned those *tejano filibusteros* loose. They're on their way home and I'm going to lose my ass."

"Not till they get back to those cattle, you haven't," Stanton protested excitedly.

"No chance, Spence. I know when I'm licked."

"I don't!"

"I want no more to do with it, the way odds stand now."

"Who the hell said anything about you?" Stanton snapped impatiently. "I don't give a damn for the odds. How much is your title from Armijo worth?"

"Nothing, the Texas side of the line, out there. Maybe this side, either. If you're thinking what I think you are, you're crazy, Spence. You don't even have a crew to move anything like a herd this size. And you don't know what you'd run into out there."

"I sure do. Two thousand longhorns. That's enough for me."

"Well, if I'm going to do business with an idiot," Wetzel said, "ten percent over what I paid the governor. Cash, *amigo,* here and now."

"My share in that inventory out there come anywhere near covering?"

Wetzel nodded. "A little over, I'd say."

Stanton calculated rapidly. He knew what Jaime's instant reaction would be. But he had to think of 'Mana, too.

"What if I bust — if the *tejanos* beat me back to the herd — or if I have to run with only a few?"

"Hell, I'm no Shylock, Spence. We'll prorate. I'm out the works, as it is. You go belly-up, I'll take half the loss. The other half's yours. You got to take some risk if you're going to be so bullheaded."

"Besides my neck, you mean."

Wetzel shrugged. "Fair's fair."

"The Solomon of Santa Fe," Stanton snorted. "Get off your butt and find me that wagon. I've got to get loaded and out of here."

CHAPTER NINE

Jaime Henry had known, since the day when he had first seen her when he was sixteen years old, that he was in love with 'Mana Stanton. It was total worship. With no disloyalty to Spence on the part of either of them, he thought that 'Mana had always known and understood.

Her warmth and gentleness toward him had made it more than any friendship he had ever known and a long way from the easy, half-joking, day-to-day mother-son relationship she tried to make it appear for the benefit of all. There was just not that damn much difference in age between them, in his opinion.

She was in his heart and it seemed, more often than he cared to admit, in his dreams. To that degree, she could do no wrong. But she sure graveled the hell out of him over what to do with Helga Cagle's brothers.

Although she stubbornly refused to discuss it further with him, he had the persistent feeling she had been badly used in their alkali camp on the eastward grass. Maybe coming and going, as well. The thought brought fresh fury whenever it recurred.

You stomped a snake, whether it struck or not.

111

So at least it wouldn't have the opportunity another time. That was instinct. A primal law of survival. In his book, it was natural justice, to boot. There was no other law you could turn to, here. He knew Spence Stanton would side with him as Chato did. But 'Mana would not.

Jaime's final intent had been to lock the Cagles up in the adobe he was now sharing with Amelio at the corrals and to set a guard on them to see they stayed put. Not to give Lew Cagle a chance to mend his wound. The hell with that. Let the son of a bitch do for himself with his brothers' help down there or die and be damned. Small difference, one way or the other.

Just to keep the bastards by till Spence got back. Spence had crossed tracks with them before. There was Helga and the man they had beaten to death and hanged in the malpais. 'Mana was his wife. She would confide in him. This was his ranch. Spence was a hard man when need be, but he was just. Let him decide what was to be done.

Chato grudgingly agreed. He said Utes were very good at such things and he would like to be here when *el patrón* returned. He thought that even a Ute might learn some new things from Spencer Stanton when he found these *cabrones* here. Even an old-time Ute who remembered when they still used the red-ant hills and green buckskin, tied tight and soaked in water so it would shrink excruciatingly in drying, when dealing with enemies. But 'Mana remained opposed and adamant.

To Jaime's surprise, she did not insist on caring further for the wounded man. She did not seem so much worried about the risk of further travel in his condition. She had done as much for him as she could or as could be expected. Let the rest be in the hands of God.

What she wanted was to get them out of there. She wanted them off the Corona. As soon as possible. As far as possible. Far enough that they would not return and could not. Without further violence.

In the end, Jaime was obliged to understand, even if he could not bring himself to approve. It was not these men of which she was afraid. Not now. Nor was she afraid for them, for the wounded man. Her fear, he came to realize, was of her husband. She was afraid of Spence Stanton and what he might do when he returned. When he learned what had happened. If they were still here.

She was afraid of blood on the land. Vengeance which could buy only a passing satisfaction and accomplish nothing else. He was convinced that he and Chato, probably even old Amelio and Raul Archuleta and his boys as well, would catch their hiding from Spence for allowing it, but he finally agreed to do as she asked.

Chato's Utes made a stretcher of hide, laced to two slender poles. Slings were rigged so it could be swung from two saddles, one on either side. They discharged the Cagles' guns and put them with their other weapons in the pack on their lead horse. They made Matt and Zeke Cagle lift their wounded brother onto the stretcher. It was slung between his own riderless horse and that ridden by Zeke, leaving Matt free to manage the packhorse and choose the way after they were freed.

'Mana came out with a jar of the patent *Yanqui* salve and some extra bandaging. These were also put in the pack. During all of these preparations, the Cagles remained prudently silent. But when his brothers were in saddle, Lew Cagle spoke to 'Mana from the stretcher.

"I want you to know, ma'am. I'm obliged. I had to tell you."

"That's right," Matt Cagle seconded, deferentially taking off his hat. "Can't say the same for bucko-boy, there, or these damn Indians. But you been real well-meaning, missus. You done the best you could, by us, in spite. Thank your man for that. For me, personal. Maybe we can do the same for him, sometime."

'Mana was not misled.

"Mister, let me tell you something," she said quietly. "If any of you ride onto this ranch again — back into New Mexico again, for that matter — Spencer Stanton will shoot you on sight. So will any man who works for us. I'm giving that order, myself. Now."

Jaime picked up the lead of his own horse and drew 'Mana aside.

"Spence'll probably raise the roof over this,

too," he said. "I know Chato says he'll handle it, but I have to be sure they're gone. Myself. That much, at least. I have to know."

"Of course you do, Jaime," she answered gently. "I want you to. Don't worry. I'll have Raul and Mama Archuleta come up here. Benny and Ramón can look after the youngsters and the stock till you get back."

"Won't be long. Two, three days."

"Do something else for me. Soon as you're sure, return to his camp with Chato. Bring Helga back down. She's still in no shape to be up there among strangers."

Jaime nodded soberly, but he was smiling wryly to himself as he swung up. Hardly two days on the Corona and the girl from the malpais was already no longer regarded as a stranger. She was a part. These enemies were not yet out of her yard and the *patrona* was already thinking again of another's troubles. That was 'Mana Stanton.

He reined back to Chato and his waiting Utes. Together they rode out with the Cagles in their midst.

They struck the Taos trail slightly west of the foot of The Crossing over The Reef, not far from where they had buried Fergy Ferguson. The gaunt mesa towered high and forbidding above them. Leaving their prisoners surrounded by his Utes, Chato signaled Jaime and rode out of earshot.

"We could save ourselves a long ride, *amigo,*"

the Indian suggested with characteristic practicality.

"We have our orders," Jaime said.

"She is a woman. We are men. This is a good place. Used right, a Ute knife is clean and quick, and they'd never be found."

The same temptation was strong upon Jaime, but he shook his head regretfully.

"I know," Chato argued earnestly. "But I am thinking of her. And the *señor*. It is the only way to be sure."

"We'll do the best we can," Jaime said. "Blindfold them. Tie their hands down short, so they can't slip the blinders. No use letting them learn the shortcut over The Crossing, anyway."

Chato shrugged with strong disapproval.

"I don't understand you *extranjeros*," he complained. "*Yanqui* and *mexicano*, it's all the same. You don't learn how it is in this country, as the Ute has. You live, but not by letting your enemies do so. That is the road to death. "We know that. So we have lived here a long time. It is the only way."

"Hell, I know that!" Jaime growled. "I've stayed alive a spell, myself. First time I saw these bastards, I wanted to gut-shoot the lot and wish I had. But I don't make the rules. Not on the Corona. And neither do you. Get those blinders on. Right."

Chato rode back to his men, switching to his own tongue to give the order. Jaime sat crook-legged in his saddle, relishing the quick fear which came up in the eyes of the prisoners at the unknown Ute words.

"Damn it," Matt Cagle protested in thin alarm as Utes reined in against his horse on each side with short, braided lengths of rawhide like pigging-strings in their hands. "This ain't what the missus ordered!"

"Didn't order accidents, either," Jaime said harshly. "But they can happen and sure as hell will if you don't shut your yap."

Matt Cagle subsided. The last Jaime saw of their eyes, they were rolling in terror of the unknown as their own neck cloths were folded over them and jerked to a tight knot behind. Certain that the prisoners could see nothing and that their short-tied wrists would let the two in saddle handle their animals without being able to reach the blindfolds, Jaime signaled the party on.

Chato took the lead, now. Automatically. Without question, as befitted a chief and the son of a chief. Amused, Jaime did not deny him the instinctive arrogance, and the Ute made his own malicious game of his leadership. Before they had covered the half-mile or so to the foot of The Crossing, he had led them through so many convolutions and changes of direction that no sightless man would retain even the vaguest notion of course and direction.

The increasing tenseness and rigidity of the two mounted prisoners betrayed their growing uncertainty and anxiety. Jaime watched the sweat run from beneath their blindfolds with wicked enjoyment.

Once, when Matt Cagle instinctively tried to raise a tethered hand to swab it away, Jaime was instantly close in beside him, the point of his belt knife jabbed deeply enough into the Cagle's hide over his kidney to be sharply felt. The man grunted, stiffened even more, and thereafter was exceedingly careful that any other necessary limited move could not be misinterpreted.

Chato grinned back in approval, and then they started up the relatively smooth trace of The Crossing, itself. The Ute and his men rode so that although they, themselves, traveled the best going, the Cagles were jostled aside wherever possible so that their animals had to take the worst footing, to the frequent, jolting punishment of their riders.

For a while the sun was hot in the defiles through which The Crossing threaded in its ascent of the great barrier face of The Reef. Chato held steadily on, deliberately passing the occasional small streams which watered the way, grinning back at Jaime as the blindfolded heads of the thirsty men turned hopefully toward the sound of the cold, running water. The afternoon dragged out into dusk without a slowing of the pace.

It was more than an hour after full dark before Chato halted in a narrow place, where even the stars were blanked out, to let the saddle-weary prisoners relieve themselves. Jaime saw that Lew

118

Cagle, helpless on the stretcher between the two horses, had given up some time before and wet himself copiously. The tremendous streams puddled by the other two when they were unlashed and permitted to briefly dismount were satisfying proof of the intense discomfort of physical restraint to which they had been forced to subject themselves.

Remounting and lashing the Cagles as before, Chato put the cavalcade in motion, again. Night chill set in. Jaime freed his jacket from his cantle and pulled it on. Its warmth was welcome. Chato glanced back at him in question. Jaime shook his head. There were jackets in the Cagles' pack and blankets for the wounded man, but Jaime was relishing Chato's way. The hell with them.

They crossed the summit of The Reef a little after midnight and began the twisting descent of the tilted, long-slanting north wall of the great mesa. At first light, they reached a trickle tributary of the Purgatoire and stopped to let their horses thirstily nuzzle water which would presently run into the Arkansas and in good time to the big bend where the trail cut up to the Smoky Hill and on to the Missouri.

They resumed along this without allowing their prisoners to dismount or water. Jaime signaled the Utes to drop back, one by one, until only Chato and himself remained in escort. At a suitable place, just emerging from a thick stand of sapling timber growing from the deadfall tangle of an old burn, the two rode close to the mounted men and cut the short ties which restricted the use of their arms and hands.

Wheeling, Jaime and Chato rode smartly back into the thicket and pulled up there, hidden, to watch. The Cagles pulled up at once, slipping their blindfolds as quickly as possible. They seemed surprised to find themselves alone and narrowly searched their surroundings. When they could discover no sign of their escort, they flung down by the creek and drank deeply. Matt carried water to his wounded brother in his hat, and while Lew thirstily refreshed himself, Zeke broke into their pack for their weapons.

Rearmed, they mounted and resumed on down the creek. Jaime and Chato watched until they were sure the three would continue to follow the water. In three days they could reach Bent's Fort, in three weeks the River towns, if the wounded man improved enough to stand the pace. It was not likely they would turn back. Nothing was to be gained. The Reef barred their way. It was a long, dry detour out onto the *jornada* to bypass it, and they knew the reception which would be waiting, should they attempt to return.

Jaime and Chato reined after the other Utes, back toward the hidden northern entrance to The Crossing.

Chato's lower camp at this season was up a side draw, three or four miles into the spectacularly palisaded shelter of the canyon of the Cimarron. Helga came hurrying down from the Ute wickiups with some of the children to meet them as they rode in. Except that her lacerated feet yet hurt her some and she limped a little in her haste, Jaime saw with approval that she moved as the children did, unself-consciously and animal-free. Her movement was a delight to watch.

She ran to his knee, gripping it insistently and looking anxiously up at him.

"Chato got there in time?" she demanded. "She's not hurt? They're dead?"

The questions were staccato with concern. He smiled reassuringly down at her.

"The *patrona*'s fine. It's all right."

He saw the quick flood of her relief and regretted the rest he must admit.

"So are your brothers, worse luck. We hauled them over the mesa and dumped them loose on the edge of the plains, pointed east with hell in their hip pockets to keep them going."

"Loose!" she protested incredulously. "Why you stupid, wobble-kneed damned fool!"

"Her orders, miss."

"Christ, what's somebody like her know about bastards like them?" she demanded angrily. "What the hell's the matter with you — been gelded, or something — no guts of your own? I wish to God the mister'd been there. He'd knowned what had to be done and he'd done it!"

Her furious scorn stung like a lash. She turned heel and walked off toward the camp, avoiding him without turning her head when he tried to ride up again beside her. Chato was watching and Jaime saw he was grinning. That stung as well.

He couldn't figure this girl. Bad-mouthed enough, lord knew. Maybe all she'd ever heard. A harsh, rough way about her. A bitter one. Most ways hardly a proper woman. So damned much bedrock flint and steel in so soft a case. Yet so much different than the three sons of bitches he and Chato had dumped off on the Purgatoire. It seemed impossible they could have borned in the same bed.

Still, stock bred out that way, sometimes. There'd be a scrub calf or foal dropped every now and then that there was no accounting for at all. Different conformation, different coat and eye and lift of head. Better blood, for some blamed reason. And it was a slow process. But it was these they picked up and nursed and kept apart and bred again in time to improve the line. Somehow it worked, most of the time.

"Get your possibles," he told her. "We're going home."

And he pulled up to wait.

Sunset came early, this close to the mountains. At the point out on the grass where they must branch south from the Cimarron, Jaime pulled up to water their horses. He flopped down wearily on streambank grass a rod upcurrent. He had been a long time in the saddle without sleep or rest. He drank and doused his face refreshingly in the frigid water. Rising to his knees, he pulled out the tail of his shirt and dried.

When he tucked the shirt back in, Helga was also nuzzling in the stream beside him. She sighed, satisfied, slid back a little, and rolled over, turning her face up to the red gold left over the peaks by the vanished sun. The sky color touched highlights in the soft gold of her hair and warmed her cheeks and struck slumbrous flame from the depths of her eyes.

He leaned over and kissed her gently. It didn't mean much of anything. Just something he wanted to do on the spur of the moment. She didn't protest at all. Just opened her mouth and maliciously bit his lip. Not enough to draw blood, but good and hard just the same. Angered, he bore back down then, kissing the hell out of her for real.

She still didn't struggle. For a brief breath he felt something he never had before. Then she put the palm and fingers of one small hand up to his cheek, hooked her nails, and raked them down the length of his jaw. He sat back in genuine astonishment, hand to face, and discovered blood oozing from four long scratches. She still lay motionless, looking unblinkingly up at him with no reaction at all that he could see.

"I didn't exactly mean to do that," he protested.

She still made no other response and again anger flashed in him.

"At least you know I ain't been gelded!" he growled.

"Maybe," she agreed soberly. "And I don't give a damn."

She rose to her feet. Jaime followed her to the horses. They mounted and continued out onto the grass in silence.

Once, when they were already within sight of the Corona house, Jaime thought he wanted to tell her something. But he wasn't a bit sure that he didn't want to belt her one, too, so he held his peace.

CHAPTER TEN

Stanton discovered that his wagon was the first four-wheeled vehicle to enter the yard at Mora in the two hundred years there had been Peraltas on the rancho. There was incredulity that he had experienced no more difficulty than that he had needed better brakes on some down-stretches of Glorieta and the wheelers Wetzel had provided were too light for the work expected of them on heavy grades or deep going.

Don Felipe was fascinated with the simple expedient of the water barrel he had fastened to the outside of the off sideboard between fore and aft wheels so he could stop where the day ended and get the most of travel light without seeking nearest water. Josefina, the fat Mora cook, was intrigued with the cupboard he had arranged as he jolted along, so that with the endgate lowered to horizontal, a camp kitchen of sorts and a work table were ready at the slip of a hasp. And 'Lardo, the wolf, was impressed that with the wagon Stanton had made nearly as good time up from Santa Fe as an unencumbered man in saddle might expect on the long haul.

But the biggest excitement was over 'Mana's pregnancy. The childless old don insisted a fiesta was in order. Stanton was able to evade this only when he learned 'Lardo had not found the Cagles at Taylor Springs. Obviously, if they had not doubled back to water there, as Stanton had expected, and with one of them wounded, they would have had to hole up, at least temporarily, at next nearest water.

This would certainly have to be someplace on the Corona, even possibly at the ranch, itself. Under cover of the real urgency of this fact, he was able to borrow the company of 'Lardo and five of the best armed of the Mora *vaqueros* for such time and services as he might require.

He traded the too-light wheelers Wetzel had provided for the wagon for a less tractable but much heavier, big-shouldered team from the Mora corrals. With a layover of little more than an hour and time to find a big, newfangled spring-wound kitchen clock as a present for Josefina, he was out of Mora with his escort, northbound along the base of the mountains on the old Indian trade-trail for the Corona.

They drove late, slept briefly, and pushed on, Stanton and 'Lardo each thinking their own thoughts, wanting to find the Cagles and hoping they would not. At midmorning, their impatience grew past confining. Leaving the *vaqueros* to bring the laden wagon on, they pushed ahead to the limit of their horses, hammering in dusted and sweaty to the Corona yard well before dark.

Stanton knew at once that something had happened in his absence. Some diversion from the normal course of events. He had left Jaime orders regarding the house addition. But the results of only two good days of work or less were all that was apparent.

They rushed to him before he was dismounted. They told him in the excited way of people at homecoming. Each cut in upon the other, trying to set the record straight according to his own views and impressions and so confusing accounts more than need be. But he grasped the important facts.

The Cagles. Their plea for help. 'Mana's attempt to do what she could and believed she must. Going onto the grass with Matt Cagle to keep him from discovering Helga's presence. The forced return to the house and the intent behind it. Jaime's intervention and Chato's, and the final disposition.

Stanton disapproved of some of what had been decided and done, because it would not have been his way. But he said nothing of that because he had not been present. What pleased him was that each here, faced with unexpected danger and decision, had made a reasoned judgement and acted upon it, each in his own way. And in the end, they had acted together to overcome the threat as best they could.

He had long known this would become a necessity if the ranch was to survive. It was the first reassuring indication he had seen that the Corona, even as short-handed as it was, could defend itself in his absence. It lifted a burden from him. In times to come, he could not always be here or fit to fight. Nor would he live forever. No man did. The Corona could not be dependent upon one man.

He said nothing of events in his night camp at Taylor Springs. He and 'Lardo knew who had shot Lew Cagle. It now seemed valueless information which could only cause needless alarm for him in 'Mana and Jaime. Nor did he mention the unease apparent in Santa Fe or the Texas filibustering expedition the governor had intercepted and shipped off to Mexico City. These concerns, too, were not of the moment.

There was excitement over the wagon and its contents as they were carried into the house and stacked against the fireplace, which was not in use at this season. He explained that these were only those things which he could find in Wetzel's stock. The rest would be forthcoming from the River as soon as the order could be transmitted and return freight space booked.

He gave 'Mana the arrow and spear points he had found at Taylor Springs and Fergy's sewing kit. She was as excited as a little girl over the first and her eyes moistened sadly over the second. When she returned to the kitchen to expand her planned meal to feed all, he went down to the corrals with Abelardo to find a suitable bedding ground for the men from Mora.

Coming back, he found Helga waiting for him beside some chaparral obscured from both house and corral. He had forgotten he had yet to arrange some disposition for her.

"I'd just figured I'd mosey —" She checked herself, seemingly in search of better words. She resumed, speaking slowly, carefully, with great effort. "I care to walk along back with you. If you have no mind."

"No. Of course not, Helga. Something troubling you?"

"Oh, no!" she protested with an almost blinding smile. "I couldn't dream a place like this. Not even when I was little, and they mostly let me be. I mean before I knew there was any other kind of living. The way she treats me. Same as if I was another woman. Like her, a lady. I never knew how, before. But I want to learn."

Stanton smiled at her.

"Somebody as pretty as you are, it comes easy," he said.

"The hell it does!" she answered, reverting savagely. "All it means is you can't stand up for what you want, what you believe you can do. You got to lie on your back."

She checked herself again and faced him, gripping his upper arms tighter than she realized.

"God damn it, I don't mean to say it that way. Nobody's had me. But it's a wonder, far back as I can remember. Every son of a bitch you meet wanting to make his try. And nobody giving a damn but you. She knows what I'm talking about. She knows what to do about it. You're fixing to send me on someplace. I want to stay. I want to stay nearby her. I want to learn to be like that, too."

Stanton gently disengaged her grip.

"I'm afraid that's impossible," he said. "You see, Helga, Mrs. Stanton is expecting a baby in the spring —"

"All the more reason, then!" she cried, grabbing hold of him again, eagerly seizing this fresh argument and tugging insistently at him as though to implant her own urgency by physical force.

Once again he detached her grip. She stiffened defiantly.

"Christ, mister, I won't filth your house. I don't dirty my bed or anyone else's. I'm clean as any when I've got soap and a tub and washboard. Yes, and I'm decent too, by God. Whatever you and some of your menfolk think. I'll learn to talk the same. What's more, I can do more work than any son of a bitch you've got on the place!"

Her desperation was overpowering. Stanton knew what his own inclination of the moment was. But he also knew it was bad judgment. His household needed an unbedded woman no more than the Corona needed unbred heifers.

"I'm leaving again early in the morning," he said quietly. "We'll be crossing the Trail. I'll have Mrs. Stanton fix you up with what you need. We'll find somebody heading east that you can safely travel with. Believe me, you'll be better off back in your own country."

She looked at him hard for a long moment, then shrugged in dejected resignation.

"That makes it hard, mister," she said softly. "I sure as hell can't have what I ain't got. I got enough sense to know that. And you're boss here. So whatever you say."

She turned and walked quickly up the path ahead of him. He loitered a little, letting her gain a lead, ruefully smiling a little to himelf at how she had, in small bits and pieces, in spite of the pressure of her urgency, tried to speak a few phrases as she imagined 'Mana might have done. Complete even to suppression of her nasal river-bottom twang and an attempt at the soft, deep pitch of 'Mana voice. He felt, he decided, like a thoroughgoing shit.

Later, when the big kitchen table had been trestled out to full length and they were all at supper, he noted that Jaime missed much of the fellowship and what was said by others for keeping his eyes on Helga. The girl, as befitted her place and disappointment, kept her attention downcast upon her own plate except when there was need to re-serve from the stove.

Stanton thought 'Mana was watching the two as well, perhaps with a little touch of amusement, but she sat complacent, without comment, letting the girl from the lava dish and fetch as though it was a custom of the household. He wanted to comment upon the four half-healed red weals down Jaime's cheek, but no one else had done so since his arrival and he prudently did not.

When Amelio and Helga had cleared, he summoned them back to the table and a splash of *aguardiente* in a tin cup with the rest. He told them then of his plan and the two thousand head of longhorns out there on the Staked Plains. He told them of the race against time which was involved but skirted detailing the reasons for it. He only said that if it succeeded, the Corona would have the biggest herd of beef stock in New Mexico.

Jaime didn't pay much attention to Helga Cagle after that. This was the stuff of life to him. What he lived for, in his mind's eye, at least. Stanton saw the quick, high surge of excitement in him. It was instantly infectious and gripped Raul Archuleta and his two oldest boys, as well. Even old Amelio banged his cup on the table in bright-eyed, enthusiastic approval. It pleased Stanton that this high spirit was there and he regretted what he must do.

'Mana made no comment, knowing that he had not told all and waiting until he could. The wolf of Mora and his *vaqueros*, who had not yet learned what his actual need of them would be, joined the old man in a banging chorus of approval and sent the *aguardiente* around again. Stanton continued.

"I brought 'Lardo and his men up from Mora because we need more hands for this and they understand this kind of a ride better than any of you here. Except you, Jaime. I want you with me more than any. But I have to think of the Corona. I'm leaving it and everything on it to you. Do as well for me again as you just have. All of you. 'Lardo and I will handle the cattle."

The Mora crew banged their cups again. Those of the Corona did not. Stanton rose to his feet.

"Daybreak," he said. "Raul, cut us out a cavvy. Four horses for each of us. The best we have. Amelio, load the wagon. Helga can help you. Bedrolls and all loose gear, stowed snug. Food for three weeks — no, make it four. Plenty of it. Can't drive that size of herd on stringbread and bacon. And leave room on the seat for Helga. She'll be going part way with us. 'Mana, see to her needings and enough pocket money to get her back to the river or as far past as she wants to go."

Cups were emptied and the table broke up. The men filed out. Amelio and Helga began plundering the big cupboards flanking the kitchen and the new food stores he had brought up from Santa Fe. 'Mana joined them to supervise. Stanton nodded to Jaime and they went out onto the privacy of the veranda.

"Damn you, Spence," Jaime complained, "how come I always get the blunt end of the stick? There's a bit you ain't told me, ain't there?"

"Some," Stanton admitted. "I'm no way sure just how this is going to go."

"So I figured. Just how you aim to get those

133

cattle? Bid 'em in at auction or something?"

"You could say. Real reason I want you here is backup. In case their owners don't like the color of our money or the language in our bill of sale."

"You got one?"

"For what it's worth. But we may have to come humping back without a hide and a whole damned hornets' nest on our tail. I want you and the Archuletas and Amelio at hand to help swat them off, if need be. Give us fifteen days. No way to make it back before then. Keep a sharp watch east as far as the Trail. Every day after that."

"I'll get word to Chato. He could use a wagonload of corn from Turley's mill about now. They ain't the best damned farmers in the world, you know. I reckon we could afford to promise him that and a couple carcasses to pit-roast when you get back."

"Not this time."

"Good way to make sure," Jaime urged. "If need be. Sure proved that with the Cagles."

"Too much risk for the Utes," Stanton said. "This has got to be strictly white man, and I'd feel better if we were hundred percent *yanqui*."

Stanton paused, wanting to go no further than necessary but realizing that Jaime was entitled to a fair notion of what might come.

"If it blows up, it'll be a pretty big bang, I'm afraid. Maybe clear to Washington and real hell to pay. Texicans are mighty touchy these days, and they know how to make themselves heard."

"Yeah. They're real lovable, that way."

"You know the Yankee army, if it gets stirred up a little. Particularly over Indians or *mexicanos*. It's apt to fight first and ask questions after. Without too much worry about boundaries and such. We're on our own, Jaime."

"You're the boss, Spence. But I tell you here and now, if you fellows get yourselves some Texican hides and I don't, you and me just ain't going to be speaking."

"If I have to, I guess I could put up with that for two thousand more head out there on our grass."

"Reckon I could, too," Jaime said. "But I still want me one personal big-mouth, belly-busting Lone Star to nail up on my wall to look at every night before I go to sleep."

"Cheer up, *amigo*," Stanton answered wryly. "You may get obliged in spades."

He went back into the house. Amelio and Helga were packing supplies in the kitchen, ready to be carried out to the new wagon. 'Mana was in their bedroom. He joined her and she signaled him to close the door. She looked at him with level eyes as he approached her.

"You're going to steal those cattle, aren't you, Spence?" she accused quietly.

"Well, Wetzel says they're a steal, if that's what you mean," he temporized.

"That isn't what I mean and you know it."

"Call it point of view, 'Mana," he said earnestly. "I've paid for them. A mighty low price, I admit, but one a reasonable man would consider fair under the circumstances, I think. All we could afford and take the risks involved, at any rate. But some may claim I bought a piece of paper instead of a herd of beef on the hoof. If they do, I suspect there may be a little argument over that."

"Just one thing: is it honest?"

He grinned wryly at her.

"Damned if I know," he admitted. "That's where the point of view comes in. But it's sure as hell just, the way it's come about. I can tell you that. And we'll never have an opportunity like it again."

He took her arms and pulled her to him.

"Look, *querida,* some things have to be done when the time's at hand or they never get done at all. You were right about the feeling that's building in Santa Fe. The rest of the province, too, near as I can make out. Maybe in Texas and the States and the rest of Mexico. Some kind of trouble is coming. I'm pretty sure of that, now.

"If there's advantage, we've got to take it. Be damned fools not to. In a little while it may be too late."

She nodded somberly.

"I think I understand," she said. "At least as much as a woman can. If you think it's right, go with God, Spence. It's — it's just that I want no shadows, here. No regrets. Not ever. Do what you think is best. But change your orders a little."

"In what way?"

"I want Helga to stay here with me."

"She's no part of us."

"At least until the baby comes. You said I would need a woman. So does she. We'll be good for each other. She can learn to be all the help I need."

"You're thinking of her," Stanton protested. "I think of you."

"She's lonely, Spence. I have been, too, and will again. You have your work cut out for you. Even more, now. Let me have mine, too. To do in my own way. Please."

Some vague misgiving persisted in Stanton, but he saw here an easing of his conscience concerning the full-breasted waif he had found in the malpais and he nodded.

"All right, if that's what you want. Go tell her."

"I think you'll have to do that, Spence. I don't think she'd stay unless she heard it from you. And let Amelio go with you after those cattle."

"Hell, I can't do that!" Stanton protested. "There's enough against me as it is. Don Felipe's men are all I need."

"Who are you trying to fool?" 'Mana said imperturbably. "Not me. I am the Corona too, you know. Add it up — six from Mora and you makes seven. Two point riders, two swings, and two drags, with somebody to drive the wagon. Not a hand left over for emergency, even if everything goes well."

"Exactly enough, if everything goes well. So it has to."

"Nothing ever does. That well. Amelio can handle the wagon and cook, which is something you haven't counted on. And leaves you free to fill in, wherever. You need him, Spence."

"Like a rifle with a bent barrel! Good God, 'Mana, he's an old man. All broken up."

"He's exactly eleven years older than you are, Spencer Stanton. And tough enough to handle the *patrón,* himself, if I remember right."

"Be reasonable, woman."

"He'll be no good to me here, or to Jaime, really. But he's one more gun, if he can stay on the seat of the wagon. And he's part of the Corona. He wants to do something. He wants to be of use. You can't take that from him."

"Oh, Christ," Stanton said in exasperation, "I'm surprised you don't want to go, too!"

"I do," 'Mana told him sweetly, "but I'm afraid I'm not a very good thief."

CHAPTER ELEVEN

Stanton was acutely conscious of the limitations forced upon him by the small size of his crew. He therefore started organizing it at the outset into as efficient a cavalcade as possible. He knew this was the time it must be done.

In the next week or ten days, routine must become automatic and unshakable. Each man had to know precisely what his specific duties were and what was expected of him. Each had to learn to rely implicitly upon his fellows to do their share and to attend first and foremost to his own tasks in any situation. All hope of success lay wholly in how effectively they learned to work together.

He allowed Abelardo to assign himself to the head of the string. He detailed two Mora *vaqueros* to ride behind their foreman at point of the two dozen relief horses in their loose cavvy. Hopefully, on the return, they would function the same with the longhorn herd.

Two more *vaqueros* rode the flanks at swing. Amelio and the wagon followed, serving as drag as well, keeping the horses pushed along from behind. The fifth *vaquero* trailed the wagon at some distance to haze up any strays which got past Amelio and to keep a rear guard and watch.

Stanton found himself grateful that 'Mana had persuaded him to bring the old man. Although unfamiliar with any vehicle but the high, solid-wheeled, single-axle *carretas* of Mexico, Amelio proved to be an exceptional driver, handling and saving his double-up team with ease. And, as 'Mana had suggested, his presence freed Stanton to keep an eye on all and to navigate.

This was the most critical responsibility. Particularly on this eastbound push. Wetzel had secured Stanton a tracing from a provincial map in the archives at Santa Fe which purported to locate the official border with Texas and upon which the governor himself had marked where he believed the confiscated longhorns were being held. But the map was without landmarks and Stanton considered its accuracy suspect.

The easiest and most logical route into the *llanos estacados* and back onto the high grass along the base of the Sangre de Cristos was obviously to follow the sure grass and water in the valley of the Canadian. Stanton supposed this had been the route followed by the filibusterers out of Texas until they were intercepted by Governor Armijo's forces and likely the one they had intended to follow later with their cattle. From where the Canadian made its big bend to swing from south to east, Stanton thought it was barely fifty miles across to the Pecos and so practically into Santa Fe itself.

He was reasonably certain he would find the longhorns somewhere along the Canadian near where it crossed the Texas border at about the 103rd meridian, a little north of the 35th parallel. But in spite of this and the surety of water and grass, the Canadian was no good for his present purpose on two counts.

It was too long and meandering a route when time was as critical as it was now. And its very obviousness made it a poor return route when pursuit was possible and even likely. He therefore was determined to drive a bee-line course for where be believed the cattle to be, marking a practical return route as they went so that if they were able to secure the cattle, they could get them deep back into New Mexico in the shortest possible time.

Stanton was able to locate usable water at adequate intervals early on, and it was not difficult to maintain a generally direct line as long as they had the mountains in view behind them. But as the white crests turned blue with distance and sank below the western horizon, the incredibly flat monotony of the Staked Plains engulfed the cavalcade.

The vast level was awesome, confusing the senses. It was a sea of wiry, alkaline grass in every direction, with seldom even an occasional stunted clump of brush to draw the eye, so that there was often no reliable way to even orient the sun in the constant effort to maintain precise direction. Stanton began to doubt the wisdom of his decision to cut straight across.

When they were still in occasional cottonwood bottoms country, now far behind, he had ordered a taut hammock of stout tarpaulin lashed under the wagon bed above the running-gear. The original idea had been for each man in saddle to salvage scattered firewood as they encountered it, tossing it onto the stretched tarp against later fuel shortage. In some stretches it now became necessary to sort out the longer sticks in this reserve and plant them upright at suitable intervals so that by sighting back they could maintain a reasonably straight line of travel. Stanton wondered if the *llanos estacados* had not gotten that name from a similar expedient employed by some early Spanish explorer.

As a further check, Stanton kept them moving after they lost the sun until they could have the reassurance of the first stars that they had not drifted too far to the left or right during the day. As a result of this they were twice forced to overshoot available water and so were obliged to camp dry. But in both instances he was able to locate buffalo wallow sinks before next mid-morning which contained enough white-rimed water yet sweet enough for the animals.

In spite of the scarcity of water in any quantity, Stanton was surprised by the generally good quality of the grass on the *llanos*. It was not the rich fodder of the Corona, but it, too, cured on the stalk for year-round feed, and he thought that in time, perhaps with wells to supplement natural runs and catchbasins, stockmen could prosper here. However, he found the almost complete absence of wildlife curious.

There was ample evidence that buffalo had once been present in great numbers, but the most recent sign he could discover was old. Perhaps twenty years or more. And with the bison, other grazing game and the predators which preyed on them had disappeared as well. He supposed some persistent drouth of the past had driven them north or closer to the mountains. For nearly a hundred miles the cavalcade had sighted only a few whistling colonies of curious prairie dogs and an occasional hawk or owl against the evening sky.

He was therefore startled as they hunkered about their supper fire on the fifth evening out from the Corona to hear coyotes yapping in the distance. Abelardo shook his head.

"Perros," the wolf of Mora corrected. "Mexican sheep dogs. They have not learned to sing as well as the wild ones, but they try when the moon is right."

"Sheep dogs? Way to hell and gone out here?"

"And sheep, *señor. Los pastores.* The lonely ones. I have been expecting to find one of their camps for some time. They started coming up from Mexico and out here from the mountains a long time ago. Before the time of Don Felipe's father, I think. Or his grandfather.

"They find a little water and make a little farm

143

and graze their sheep. They have no enemies here, you see. Only sometimes a little trouble with the Comanches, maybe. For sheep the grass is good and no one else troubles them."

"How many of them are there?"

"*Quien sabe?* I do not think they know, themselves. Maybe ten, twenty flocks — ten or twenty families — in all of the *llanos*. It is not a life for everyone. But that singing is a good sign. We will ride there, tomorrow. We must be near where those *tejanos* left their cattle, now. *Los pastores* will know where they are. They know all things on the *llanos*. They will know the way and where to find water. They are very poor, *señor*. A little beans and bacon will buy much from them."

Stanton felt relief that much needed information might be available, but he could not keep from scowling at the Peralta foreman.

"Damn it, 'Lardo, you might have told me we might find help out here!"

Abelardo shrugged.

"You did not ask."

Stanton rolled in and slept heavily, the distant yapping music in his ears.

He awoke at first light to gun-sound from the same direction as the evening serenade.

The concussions had a peculiar rhythm. Each was immediately preceded by a faint, popping explosion, followed with a slight lag by the roar of the main charge. He knew he was listening to the fire of old smoothbore flintlock muskets, the first sound being the flash of powder in the priming-pan. And by the measured intervals between each discharge, he thought there were three such weapons, being fired as rapidly as their owners could recharge and reprime the cumbersome pieces.

The absence of return fire betrayed something else. The muskets were opposed to silent weapons. Indian arrows.

"Comanches!" Abelardo shouted as they jerked on boots and ran to their horses, *"Ándale!"*

Detailing one Mora *vaquero* to remain with Amelio to keep the cavvy of relief horses bunched and protected, Stanton and Abelardo, with the four other Mora riders, swung up saddles, bridled, and rode hard toward the sounds of firing.

Stanton found the ride a curious and unreal sensation. The gunfire was obviously close at hand, yet the *llanos* appeared to extend unbroken to the vague eastern horizon, with no movement or threat in sight. Then, suddenly, barely a mile from their camp, the great plain opened into a yawning void. A wide ravine lay before them, cutting a serpentine course through the grass, invisible until the last moment because both lips were of the same height and coloration.

On the floor was the meander of a shallow, sandy stream, forming a series of green benches between its loops. On the largest of these was a clutch of small, sod-roofed adobe shacks. The musket fire came from ports in the thick walls of one of these. It was directed at a dozen or more mounted Indians who were circling under cover of the cutbank of the stream, keeping the defenders pinned within their own walls while several more Indians were dismounted in a flock of sheep on the next bench, slaughtering and skinning out as many half-grown lambs as they could conveniently lay hand to.

A talus slope ran down the near ravine wall where an undercut had caved in. Its initial roughness had weathered and been powdered smooth and deep with dust by the sharp hoofs of many sheep in repeated passage, up and down. Stanton took his party down this without slacking. He bore for the attackers ringing the adobes. Abelardo and his men from Mora, better understanding the most practical need for the moment, rode for those among the sheep.

At the first shot, the mounted Indians surrounding the bench containing the adobes dropped quickly downstream toward the butchers in the flock. Under cover of this support, the skinners each grabbed up an unskinned carcass and the hides they had already flayed and ran for their horses in the cutbank at the far end of the bench. Slinging the carcasses and hides across their knees ahead of their saddle pads, holding them in place with their forward-leaning bodies, the butchers raced off down the shallow stream.

One of the retreating attackers leaving the adobes hit a sand hole in the stream bed, just as he disappeared beyond a twist of the cutbank, and his horse fell with him. Stanton did not see him hit the surface, but the geyser of water he flung up sprayed above the cutbank. Thinking his fall might have momentarily stunned the Comanche and that the Indian might be another source of valuable information, Stanton rode hard down the stream, passing himself from the view of the Mora crew.

As he rounded the sheltering turn of the cutbank, here eight or ten feet high, he came so abruptly upon the fallen horse, just thrashing to its feet, that he had to pull hard into a rearing halt to avoid entangling his own mount. Tilting sharply aside and forward in his saddle to peer past the animal's upflung head to locate the spilled Comanche, he was struck hard on the back and side by a flying body and he realized the Indian had scrambled at least part way up the side of the cutbank to leap upon him from there.

His forward-leaning position saved him, throwing the Indian a little off. The Comanche's knife slashed Stanton's riding vest from collar to armhole along the shoulder seam without drawing blood, rather than plunging into his back as intended. The Comanche's flying weight carried them both forward in a somersaulting dive into the water.

In midair, without time to clear his belt gun, Stanton reached overhead to seize the Indian's knife arm at the wrist with one hand and a fistful of hair with the other. Pulling savagely forward and down, tucking his own head as far as he could, Stanton flung the Comanche forward over his own shoulders so that the Indian's body was beneath his own when they hit the water. The bottom was close to the surface where they landed and even with this cushion, Stanton was jolted hard.

The Indian fell partially on his extended and momentarily pinioned knife arm, and with a surge of relief Stanton felt the weapon imbed itself in the bottom and tear from the Comanche's grasp. Then he was under water, the Indian twisting atop him in swift reversal to pin him down and hold his face under.

Stanton considered himself a powerful man, usually at an advantage at close quarters, and he was astonished at his inability to dislodge his adversary by sheer force. The Indian was a superb specimen, very fast, and his half-naked body was slippery in the roiled and muddied water.

Caught short of breath by the initial impact, Stanton was quickly desperate for air. He blew snortingly, as though choking, and with spasmodic effort attempted to roll opposite to his first try. Meeting expected resistance, he snapped instantly back, forcing the Comanche spread-eagled over him to fork his legs even wider to counteract the twist. At the same time, Stanton dug one bootheel into the muck of the bottom for purchase and jackknifed the other knee up into the Indian's groin, literally ramming the man's body from him.

The Comanche shuddered convulsively at the impact and doubled up on his side in a tight knot of agony as Stanton rolled clear and floundered to his feet. He stumbled against the lost knife with his boot. Seizing it, he grabbed the Indian by his floating hair and jerked him bodily to his feet. Lips drawn back tight from his open mouth in the agony of the moment, humped forward in a spraddle-legged half crouch and cradling his bruised gonads with both clutching hands, the Comanche shook the water from his eyes and looked defiantly at the knife in Stanton's hand.

With great effort, the Indian slowly straightened, waiting for the poised weapon to strike. Stanton saw the man was utterly without fear and that no satisfaction or information would be had of him, even in death. In spite of the anger and adrenalin still driving his breath from him in short explosions of sound, Stanton could not make the stroke.

Instead, he reached suddenly and caught a fancily braided and beaded hair decoration or sash which hung down the side of the Indian's right leg from the belt of his leggings to well below the knee. Stanton slashed this free. Then, with a gesture not wholly comprehensible to himself, he thrust the knife back into the man's belt.

The Comanche remained motionless for a moment, staring at him expressionlessly, then turned away. Walking painfully spraddle-legged but erect and with as much dignity as he could summon, he splashed across to his horse. Hauling himself up onto his saddle-pad, he kicked his horse up into a run downstream after his companions.

Stanton looked up and saw Abelardo and two *vaqueros* on the cutbank almost above him. They watched the Indian go but made no attempt to stop him and Stanton realized they had seen at least a part of the wordless exchange between them. Supposing he would have to answer for freeing the Comanche, he retrieved his hat and rifle, remounted, and found a way up the cutbank to rejoin his companions.

To his surprise, Abelardo grinned at him in congratulation.

"*Muy fuerte,*" the Peralta wolf said. "*Muchos cojones!*"

The *vaqueros* seemed to agree with him. Together they rode back to the largest of the Mexican sheepherders' shanties. The *pastores* were waiting in the dooryard, their three old blunderbuss muskets among them. Stanton saw they were all of one family.

There was one very old woman who was treated by the others with obvious veneration and respect. Two graying men appeared to be her sons. A father and uncle, Stanton thought. There were three younger grown men and women equivalent to each of the males. The rest were a gaggle of children of all ages which appeared to represent the fourth generation here in this wilderness.

Some of these were freeing sheepdogs from another shanty where they had been whistled in and locked up for safety when the Comanche attack came. To lose a few sheep was one thing. To lose a trained dog was catastrophe.

As Abelardo had said, these people were shy before strangers, particularly in the face of Stanton's lighter color. His courtly Spanish did little to ease that. They were very poor. Persons and surroundings attested to this. But they were very grateful.

They explained that in recent years — since the last of the buffalo had disappeared from the *llanos* — some bands of Comanches had developed a fancy for lambskin sleeping robes and saddle-pads. Some had even cultivated a taste for the roasted meat as well. Sporadic raids like the one these welcome *extranjeros* had broken up had become part of their life on the Staked Plains.

Los indios did not raid to kill the *pastores* or pillage and burn, as they did with *yanquis,* wherever they could be found at the right odds, for who would then raise the sheep for them to flay and butcher when they were hungry and cold? But it was a hard thing to be unable to satisfactorily defend oneself and to lose thirty or forty half-grown lambs, even once or twice a year. The *llanos* were unkind enough as it had always been without these thieving enemies as well.

The old woman was greatly intrigued by the sash Stanton had slashed from the belt of the

Comanche he had faced. She treated it with great respect, fingering the many intricately beaded and braided strands of hair.

"El gran cacique," she said. *"El Acero, en persona. Un hombre mas importante. Estos son muchos trofeos de guerra."*

From this Stanton learned that his adversary had been Iron Head, as he thought it best translated, a great Comanche chief. And the sash he had stripped from the Indian was woven of the scalplocks which were his trophies of war.

The *pastores* also knew of the longhorns he was seeking. They were amazed at the accuracy of his navigation across the *llanos*. He realized he had experienced great luck. As near as he could determine, he had missed but two of the dependable water supplies available along the course he had taken, and he was told how to locate even these on the return trip.

This ravine was the home camp of this clan, at what they called the bluffs of the *llanos*. The uncertain stream which coursed it ran within a few miles into the Rio Colorado, which he identified as the Canadian. They had no notion as to where the Texas-New Mexico border lay hereabouts, since in the time of the eldest it had all been one country. But they thought it was nearby, perhaps two or three miles in one direction or the other.

For several months now, big-horned cattle had been held by a small crew where the ravine ran into the river. The *pastores* did not understand and cared little for the bill of sale Stanton had acquired, no matter how speciously, from Governor Armijo. It was enough for them that he was of New Mexico and so a countryman by whatever bond the country gave them.

The *tejanos,* like those with the cattle, were a bad lot whenever they ventured onto the *llanos.* Worse even than the thieving Comanches. A few dozen lambs were not enough for them. They wanted the water and so the land.

Those sheep on the next bench down the ravine were but one of the flocks this clan ranged. They had others within a radius of ten miles, methodically mowing the grass to the sod as they grazed and cutting their imprint into the earth for all time. So they had many for which to care.

At this dry season of the year they would have most in the wet bottoms where the ravine joined the Canadian, but this was not now possible with all those cattle there. They were shepherds, not warriors. Those three muskets were all the firearms they owned. And they were short of powder, as always.

But it would be of use to them to have those cattle gone. If it was in the minds of these *extranjeros* who had driven off the Comanche raiders also to do this, they would be happy to help to the best of their poor ability in repayment. It was a good partnership in which both parties could benefit.

Stanton thanked them in the best of his hard-learned old-world Spanish and kissed the wrinkled hand of the *vieja* and drew a map as he understood the local terrain in the dust of the dooryard, and they all squatted about it. He did not know if he was in fact the thief 'Mana had charged, but he saw no reason not to be a strategist to the best of his ability when opportunity afforded.

CHAPTER TWELVE

Heggie Duncan stood six and a half feet without his boots. He had tufted red fur on his shanks and belly and great barrel chest to match the rusty flame of his square-trimmed beard and long, unruly mane. The blood of wild Scottish chieftains was in his veins, and the turbulent, roistering godlessness of Auld Clootie himself was in his heart.

He believed himself fair in judgment and took some pride from that, and he had a forgiving tolerance in most things for the misguidance of lesser men. But he feared no living creature, man or beast, and he would abide no crap from any source without avowed repayment to the last farthing in kind and coin, devil take the hindmost.

He sat on his great dappled stallion, a full eighteen hands at the shoulder, and watched a small, long-traveled file of dusty men ride through the grazing cattle below toward the herders' camp on the riverbank. Four of them he knew well. He had ridden far and waited long for them. Once they had been friends, companions, comrades in arms. Texicans, as he was himself, by adoptive right and a certain unstinted price in blood and sweat. Heroes, even, by some counts, if it came to that.

155

They had been with Old Ben Milam at San Antone and with Sam Houston on the wily, vengeful long retreat from Gonzales to the battlefield at San Jacinto. They had raised the Lone Star flag at Washington-on-the-Brazos and helped elect The Raven president of the Republic. With independence they had enriched themselves with many a buccaneering Mexican cattle hunt across the Rio Grande. But they had tried to cheat Heggie Duncan, and now they were here. So the reckoning was at hand. The thought was pleasurable.

He spoke to the stallion and rode unhurriedly down-slope into the open. They saw him coming and recognized him from afar. He grinned at the scurry with which they prepared for him, whistling in the herders so that they were twelve in all when he rode into the camp. Twelve armed and wary men. And their wariness would betray them, for it was not rooted in sensible prudence but in fear. Fear of one man.

Such fear was unreasoning and self-destructive. Four of them should know this as well as they did the long history of their own misdeeds. But they also knew Heggie Duncan. That was his surest weapon. It always had been.

He pulled up before them, a big man on a big horse. He offered no greeting but let them look long at the two big brass-mounted percussion revolvers at his belt and the two more in saddle holsters laced to the skirt with their butts raked forward on either side just under the bow of the cantle, almost at his hip pockets.

The weapons were carefully loaded as was prudent when the necessity was to kill dangerous men. Each ball was seated in a coating of sheep tallow to seal its chamber for harder shooting. A plug of tallow was placed over each in the forward end of the cylinder to keep the ball tightly seated, however rough the going or handling, and to lubricate the lands and grooves of the barrel ahead of the lead for longer range and flatter trajectory. No man was better than his weapons and their charges.

When he thought they had seen enough to fully understand, Heggie Duncan smiled at the herders and the others who were lined up before him with the four men he had traced the long way up from the breaks of the Brazos.

"Reckon well, laddies, for you na ken me as well as those you work for do," the Scotsman warned. "I come on business and I'd as soon jawbone it out, if I'm let. But I've a load for each of you. Two, if need be. And the will, with not even a wee twitch of conscience."

They took this and he saw that they believed him. One of the four leaders stirred, temporizing.

"Oh, come off it, now!" Harper protested in his smooth and innocent way. "What's eating on you, Heggie man? Fresh met after all this time. Well met, too. We been expecting you, all along the line. We've had our times, *amigo*. You can believe that. And I reckon you've had yours. But here we are, finally together again. Like always. That's what counts. So why the hackles? That's no line for old partners to take!"

"Now, I'm glad to hear you say that, Harp," Heggie Duncan replied. "I just might be thinking otherwise, if you had not. So why don't you and Parmelee and Brazos and Sime just step out here a pace or two? Closer like. In the clear."

He waited. The four hesitated. A harder note crept into Heggie Duncan's voice.

"Nothing suits me better than old friends and kind words, but if a few hard feelings was to turn up somehow, I'd hate to see harm come to these others. I've no truck with them and it's na fair for working hands to hire on unknowing to get themselves killed for the doings of others."

He waited again, not really caring, and it showed. It was Harper who broke. He moved and the other three stepped out with him as they had been bidden. The rest of the group remained as they were.

"There's no call for this," Parmelee said with an angry note which failed to cover his anxiety. "Give the devil his due, but you're always a suspecting man, Heggie."

"Aye," Heggie Duncan agreed imperturbably, "and an unforgiving one. Look you, now. Here I am long months gone to Washington in the States to argue for annexation, as we all agreed at Bexar. There I hear how my friends have secretly marched on Santa Fe on their own and got themselves arrested and sent to prison in Mexico

City and now have been released and are on their way home."

"That's about the right of it," Sime Elliott said as earnestly as a liar could, telling the truth. "You'd have been with us if you'd been at hand."

"It was a wild scheme, I own," Harper admitted, "But to your liking, same as ours. Pushing the border on west, clean to the Rio Grande. And it would have worked if luck had been with us. We'd have had our pick of anything we wanted between here and the mountains."

"You included, naturally," Brazos Brown added quickly. "Same as if you'd been along."

"Oh, naturally," Heggie Duncan agreed again, but not as easily, for his patience was running short. "And naturally I thought of all those Mexican cattle we'd been hazing across the river for two or three years, hiding them out in the thorn thickets of the *brasada* to scratch off their Spanish brands and fatten up into good Texican stock."

"Naturally," Parmelee said.

"But there weren't even any scrubs left in those *brasada* thickets when I got there. And no message left for Heggie Duncan by his partners to tell him where they'd gone. It was na an easy trail I followed here, laddies, and I do na take kindly to it."

"Damn it, man, what's the squeak?" Harper demanded. "They're all here and then some. We picked up every stray we could lay hand to on the drive through the settlements. Worth an easy

159

twenty dollars a head somewhere on down the Canadian, and no questions asked. Share and share alike. Maybe as much as ten thousand apiece when it's done. More than any of us have made in ten years down here. So where's the hurt?"

"Here," Heggie Duncan said, banging his chest. "It's the principle. You'll none ever learn. I'll not be diddled twice in the same bed except by my own choice.

"Take your horses and go, if you're a mind. Or stay. Permanently. Right where you're standing, now. No difference. No difference at all. Either way, those beasties yonder will belong to me. All of them."

The four considered this as men will who would stop time if they could. He gave them no opportunity. He had long ago made their decision for them. His hands slapped back to the butts of the guns in his saddle holsters, saving those at his belt in case his plan went a little awry and he was knocked down or otherwise separated from his horse.

As he had anticipated, Brazos Brown's hand was faster than his skull. Amazingly faster. Brazos fired the first shot, and it was meant for the gut. It stung across Duncan's thigh with no more bite than a whiplash of brush in the *brasada*. Duncan shot him in the face and the ball tore out the back of his head.

Sime Elliott and Parmelee cleared leather almost together. He broke Sime's arm and then his back as he spun around. He fired barely enough ahead of Parmelee to deflect his shot into the ground. His own ball struck Parmelee in the groin, rupturing the great artery there so that it pumped out a pulsating urination of blood as he fell. It was a death wound but too slow for a man with a gun still in his hand. He shot Parmelee again in the head as he struck the ground.

Harper had dropped his half-drawn pistol back into its holster and jerked his arms high. There was nothing for it, now. Duncan shot him a handbreadth above the navel. Harper fell forward onto his knees, clasping both hands tight to the soft center of his body.

"Jesus Christ, Heggie!" he gasped in a hoarse whisper. He choked and buckled forward onto his face.

Duncan slid his empty gun back into its holster and took the other from his left hand, muzzle high but ever so ready to drop.

"Heggie Duncan," he said to the four herders who had been with the herd and the other four who had come out from the Brazos with the dead men. "A bad man to cross but a good one to pull with. You have a choice, which my friends here did not. We start the cattle downriver in the morning. A dollar a day and a fifty-dollar bonus, when we've sold the last head, to every man that stays on."

They did not, in fact, have a choice, as Duncan well knew. In this remote wilderness,

161

far beyond the most advanced and chancy of the Texas settlements, where could they go and how could they fend for themselves? He was not surprised when two came forward after a brief conference to say all eight were with him. He sent one back to the rim for his packhorse and went to the river to rid himself of the trail dust which had penetrated to his pores.

He had done enough for Texas. All of them had. Even the worst and most scurrilous of the footloose and the fugitive and the restless far riders who had poured down in Old Man Austin's tracks and got themselves whipped into a rag-tag army by Sam Houston, raising the rebel yell and bellowing about tyranny and human freedom and justice when the real hunger was to fill their pockets. The price was blood. They'd paid it and bought the land.

The news would have been of no use to the four now dead in the dust of the herder's camp and he had not passed it on, but he had not left Washington until the last argument had been had and the States had accepted annexation of Texas by a joint resolution of Congress. It was before a convention in the Texas capital for ratification now.

All that remained was paperwork for clerks and lawyers. In a few weeks or a few months it would become official and a practical fact, the twenty-eighth state to be admitted to the Union. If there was to be more fighting, the burden would now belong to the Army of the United

States, pressing and defending claims to United States territory. The great filibuster was over.

The time now was to fend for himself. Heggie Duncan grinned at the cattle grazing thickly across the bottoms. It had been a long time and a long ride, but he had made a fair start here today.

The settlers and the colonists, the Germans and the Swedes and the like, those sober, solid, stable people — even fighting Tennesseans like General Houston — all talked of land. But they were too damned greedy. They saw only the near mile, as was the way with small men. And their eyes were bigger than their stomachs. Hell, a single day's ride and the fact became plain enough, even to the rankest greenhorn, if he'd only bring himself to believe what he saw. Land was unimportant. There was too damned much of it in this country, and too damned much of that too poor and useless.

Cattle were something else. They were mobile, free to move, tied to no place or season, no accident of storm or drouth. They lived off the land but were not of it. It was all theirs for the taking.

Cattle. Stolen hides on the hoof. Beef, fattening on free grass. That's where the real wealth of this country was. That was where it would always be. What was sold off on opportunity for profit was easily replenished, with an obliging neighbor across the border. Particularly when the States had time to teach the greasers to mind their manners better.

Harper and Parmelee and Sime and Brazos had been a canny lot, as far as they'd thought it out. They'd come this far, all right, and then barked their shins. They'd been in too big a hurry to get to the mountains, to Santa Fe, to the fabled rich grass of that well-watered, untouched high country on out there. Not yet. Not quite yet. But pretty damn soon. Heggie Duncan was not a patient man. But he could wait. When the time was right, he would be ready.

CHAPTER THIRTEEN

Like any Texican who had fought them and stolen from them and boasted he'd had their women at will, Heggie Duncan had low regard for greasers of whatever cut of cloth. But they had one custom which had appealed to him from the start. No man could say he was indolent, or dared to, for that matter, but he relished the occasional leisure to sleep an hour in the afternoon sun.

The freedom to do so was a physical arrogance which greatly pleased him. Relaxed, his body hungrily absorbed the lazy heat, drawing energy from it which could not be received in any other way. And his mind was released to drift widely without effort. Visions of the future, unmarred by recollections of the past.

The augmented herding crew he had inherited from his partners through the simple expedient of six well-placed pistol shots was out with the beef, bunching and cutting to manageable groups to take an inventory by rough head count of what he had won in this remote and soon to be forgotten place. He was vaguely aware of their shouts to each other and an occasional bawling protest as they worked the cattle.

The air was motionless, the sun no hotter than

the need of his body for its luxuriant warmth. He lay against his bedroll with his eyes closed beneath his tilted-forward hat, contentedly traveling to far-distant places in time and space. Awareness of an intruding foreign sound came slowly. As his senses focused on it, he recognized the blatting of sheep, of all creatures second in bad-natured and malodorous complaint only to the camel.

A less cautious man would have sat up at once in astonishment and curiosity. But there was something so incongruous in the willful approach in this far distant place of a flock of woollies to a big herd of cattle, whether by human design or natural accident, that a sharp wariness seized Heggie Duncan. Without other movement, he tilted his head back a little, thus pushing the brim of his hat up with his nose so that he could see out beneath it.

Coming down the watered ravine which joined the river just above the camp and ford, powdering the air with a thin fog of dust, the sheep were being hazed along efficiently by half a dozen black and tan dogs scarcely larger than some of the lambs they drove. Duncan saw the dogs were under the control of some greaser herders, afoot on the fringes of the flock, who guided them by whistle and hand signal as necessary. The flock was a large one and with the dogs presented a scene he had not encountered since the heaths of his homeland.

A small but sturdy covered four-up wagon

emerged from the dust behind the sheep. It was driven by an old man. Six other greasers, mounted, flanked it. All were armed. Out in the lead, obviously in charge, was a tall-riding, slightly graying Yankee. It seemed an unlikely combination in this time and place. Still motionless as though sleeping, Duncan watched the approach narrowly.

The sheep came down to the ford but did not take the water. The herders and dogs checked them there, keeping them bunched but open enough to commence cropping at whatever forage was underfoot. Waiting, Duncan thought; marking time until a decision was reached.

He gave but little of a damn. If it was graze they wanted, come morning they'd be welcome to what was left. He had what he'd come for. Come sunup he'd be moving forty thousand dollars or better downriver on the hoof.

The Yankee and his party with the wagon passed the sheep and splashed across to Duncan's side of the river. The Yankee rode at an easy, unhurried walk toward where Duncan lay stretched out in the sun. The wagon and outriders behind him arched out along the riverbank. One by one they pulled up to hold individual positions, motionless, also waiting.

By the time the Yankee reached the camp, wagon and outriders formed a portion of a semicircle facing on the camp, fifty or sixty yards apart and just far enough distant to be beyond effective handgun range and still close enough

167

for their rifles to bear if necessary. A prudent man himself, Heggie Duncan did not consider the maneuver hostile, merely cautious.

He eyed the Yankee with respect as he came on, noting the brassbound Navy Colt he wore. The holster was soft with use. The man had worn it long and would well understand its purpose. Some times such notice of detail was valuable.

Duncan set his hat and came easily to his feet, unhurriedly buckling on his own belted guns. He thought it was a language the Yankee would understand and a sufficient reply to this intrusion for the moment. The Yankee smiled, pulled up at twenty feet, and stepped down, coming on afoot to extend his hand.

"Spencer Stanton, here," he offered in a fine, gentlemanly way, as though there was carpeting underfoot and clean linen and silver between them. "I run a little stock over west, near the mountains."

Duncan was startled and curious. This was not what he had expected. Men went west to the mountains, these days. Not east from them. Rivers did not run uphill.

"Aye, and do you, now?" he asked. "Santa Fe country?"

"Somewhat north," the Yankee said. "My ranch is the Corona. You may have heard of it."

"I do na ken the name. Or yours."

Spencer Stanton smiled again.

"You will."

Duncan found the surety to his liking. This was no sly and mealy-mouthing horse trader who'd have at you in one way while he was pretending another. He met the outstretched hand and matched the smile as he had a thousand others.

"Heggie Duncan," he responded. "Known about a wee mite, myself. And I run a little stock, too. Here. As you can see."

Spencer Stanton nodded.

"Two thousand head, as your men will discover when they finish making that tally out there. But you make a mistake, Duncan. Not one head of them belongs to you."

Duncan's smile broaded. So that's what it was to be. He liked the directness as well. A man played best when he knew the stakes. His eyes indicated the row of fresh mounds of raw earth a few yards away.

"Those four graves say they do," he answered. "To the last hoof and horn."

"Then the mistake is theirs," Stanton said imperturbably. "I hold a bill of sale for the lot."

He pulled a folded document from his pocket. There were two vellum sheets. The first was in a florid official Spanish script, scaled with wax and ribbon. Only a few familiar foreign words were decipherable to Duncan. The second was over the signature of a Sol Wetzel of Santa Fe. It was plain enough. It contained a translation of the first. Part was an order by the governor of the Mexican Province of New Mexico confiscating two thousand head of Texas cattle driven illegally into New Mexico by Duncan's former partners.

Each was named with others of their so-called Santa Fe Expedition, so that there would be no doubt these were the cattle in question. Next was a bill of sale for the confiscated herd, also executed by the New Mexican governor to Wetzel. Appended was an assignment of that bill of sale by Wetzel to Spencer Stanton for good and valuable consideration, all properly witnessed.

It was not in Heggie Duncan's nature to be in awe of the mechanics of any process of the law, but he judged Stanton's documents to be legal enough, as far as they went. Which was not far enough. A man had yet to stand up to Heggie Duncan with only a paper between him and the right or wrong of a matter.

This was Texas and he was Texan as much as any of those who had died at Goliad and the Alamo. Business was done more directly, here. He said so.

Spencer Stanton only shrugged. "I supposed as much," he said. "With the others as well, if I had gotten here first. In your boots, I'd probably take the same stand, Duncan. And you might make it stick, if those cattle were in Texas. But in New Mexico they're mine. I mean to have them."

"Come, now, man, you can na expect me to swallow that!" Heggie Duncan warned. "Who knows where the line is drawn out here? A plow furrow in the grass, maybe? I can put it to one side as easily as you to the other, and neither ken the truth. Or give a tinker's damn, for that matter."

"True," Stanton agreed. "But it's got to be to one side or the other."

"Look, I do na care for your greasers yonder with their long guns. If you're set to have it that way, I'll bring my own laddies in and we'll see who draws that boundary. You're 'way outnumbered, ye ken."

Stanton shrugged again.

"Maybe not. We'll have to see."

Heggie Duncan looked the calm and soft-voiced man in the eye and saw no flicker of uncertainty. Anger began to heat in him because there was no heat in Stanton. Only the same unruffled pleasantness.

"Damn it, man, you'll not be scroggin' Heggie Duncan to his face without a wee sweat and blood!" he growled.

He lifted his hat and circled it once in the air. It was a bold, brash move, calculated to burn another's powder, and he was ready for that, but Stanton's expression did not change nor did he move or tense.

Duncan's signal was seen, for one of his men yelled to the others, out among the cattle. He saw them begin to work hastily out of the stock toward the camp. He also saw Stanton's greasers dismount, even to the old man on the wagon, and fling down prone in the grass with their rifles

171

trained steadily on the camp. But Stanton remained motionless and imperturbable and there was no firing.

Instead, whistles sounded across the river. Dogs barked and raced along the fringes of the flock of sheep on the far bank. A blatting gray tide, yards wide, startled into a tight-packed, buck-jumping run, poured into the shallows of the ford. The sheep crossed quickly, scrambling up the near bank, cutting straight out toward the bluffs in a moving barrier between the cattle and the camp.

Duncan saw at once that they would cut his men off from the camp. And their blatting would drown out any orders he could give to the hands now coming down fast from the cattle. The greaser sheepherders had prudently remained on the far bank, beyond range, directing the dogs working the sheep from there. And the swiftly darting dogs were impossible marks. He jerked one of his guns and tried for the lead sheep, but those he dropped were merely overrun by those behind, and he gave up when the weapon was empty.

His men, racing in from the cattle, tried to outflank the sheep but dared not without exposing themselves to Stanton's greasers on the grass, waiting for them. They turned and tried to drive through the sheep. Duncan knew from his boyhood days that a man, even a middling small child, could quite easily make a reasonably quick way through moving sheep. But no horse, fearful of footing it could not see, could be made to more than gingerly inch its way through such a tight-packed barrier.

He jammed his spent gun into its holster, slapped the other clear, and wheeled on Stanton. The man remained as calm as before, merely shaking his head.

"There are seven rifles out there, any one of which, shooting prone like that, can put a bullet through your eyes with plenty of time to reload and help pick off your men, one by one, as they get through the sheep. And they know where the cattle are to go. So you won't save them. Or yourself. I'd drop that belt if I were you, Duncan. Slowly and carefully. So they won't misunderstand and make a mistake."

Rage shook Heggie Duncan. He had been doxied as neatly as ever a whore had cleaned his pockets when he was drunk, and by a flock of sheep. But he believed this damned Yankee about the rifles prone on the grass. No man could hold himself so coolly without speaking the truth.

Carefully, so that no gesture could be misconstrued, he dropped the gun in his hand at his feet, loosed his belts, and dropped them, too. Only then did Spencer Stanton draw his gun, gesturing with it.

"Now we'll walk out to meet your men and make them do the same. Be very sure they do, Duncan. Any mistake and I'll shoot you first. In the back."

In helpless fury, Heggie Duncan moved toward the barrier of sheep, Spencer Stanton and his gun close behind him. Whistles sounded across the river as soon as they began to move. The swift-moving dogs instantly eased their pressure on the sheep and as before, compression eased from the flock and as it opened up the stupid animals began to feed again, letting the horses of his men on through.

There was no need for an order to any of the riders. They dropped their guns at his feet as they rode up and sat waiting.

"The horses, too, Duncan," Spencer Stanton said. "We can't move these cattle too fast and we don't want you following us. So you'll have to hoof it down the Canadian to the first settlement. It's a fair ways, I know, but you can pick up your guns when we're gone. You'll have water as long as you stay on the river, there should be plenty of game, and there are enough of you so the Comanches will leave you alone."

Duncan's men dismounted. Stanton's greasers swung up and came in with the wagon. They unsaddled the surrendered horses, loaded the saddles in the wagon, and loosed the animals to trot out to the cavvy near the cattle. The old man driving the wagon took it back to the ford, crossed and disappeared up the ravine beyond, the way it had come.

Stanton signaled the Mexican herders across the river and they crossed diffidently to him. Duncan watched him thank them and send a man among the beeves to shoot a fat young animal for their use. He came back presently to Duncan and took a pouch from his saddlebag.

"We fight for what we have a right to on the Corona," he said. "But we lay no hand where we don't have the right without fair exchange."

He tossed the pouch to Duncan, who caught it sullenly. It was heavy with minted metal.

"That should cover the horses and saddles," Stanton continued. "And more than you have coming. Any complaint?"

Duncan shook his head. A man did not complain when his face was in the dirt. He ate it and held his peace. But when he got to his feet again, he did a hell of a lot more than just spit it out. A Duncan, at least. Or a Heggie. And he was both. Those Mexican mountains were not so damned far. And there were many ways to get there.

Spencer Stanton reined away and joined his greasers. They looped down to the cattle and started them moving. Heggie Duncan lay again in the sun against his bedroll and watched them stream down across the ford and up into the ravine on the other side. His men hunkered nearby, fearing his mood and awaiting his orders. He knew the time had come for words, however difficult acceptance was to come by, and he sat up.

"Laddies," he said, "that is one smart and tough and smooth-moving son of a bitch. One of these soon days, Heggie Duncan is going to find out just what color he bleeds. There's a couple of bottles yonder in my pack. Break them out and we'll have us a drink to that, God damn his soul!"

CHAPTER FOURTEEN

Abelardo and the Mora *vaqueros* had little difficulty with the cattle in crossing the Canadian ford. But it was a different matter when they started up the ravine beyond. Once they'd been forced to turn their backs on the river, a characteristic, contrary streak of obstinate cussedness surfaced. They began to break in small bunches or individual sorties at every opportunity, attempting to turn back.

In a few minutes Abelardo and his horse were both in a sweaty fury of exasperation and the *vaqueros* and their mounts were scarcely better off. Stanton knew what the difficulty was at once. Many otherwise competent and even expert stock handlers, with the contempt of lifelong familiarity, failed to give range beef its due for animal intelligence and a will of its own.

It was a common mistake among those who lived in a saddle, even in the more tranquil and mannerly bluegrass country of his own beginnings, to suppose that because of its indispensable usefulness, the horse was the intellectual king of the beasts. And it simply was not so. Even swine, for all their sloth, were more intelligent than the horse and showed it in their willful disregard for most aspects of the domestication process.

These brush-scarred cattle, for all their wild state, were descendants in part of fighting Spanish bulls bred through countless generations to keenness and courage which made them formidable adversaries for the bravest and most skilled matadors of all time. That spirit of contention was deeply imbedded beneath their ragged coats. A man had only — by carelessness or accident — to find himself afoot among them to discover this.

This ex-Mexican and now ex-Texan herd was trail-wise after the long drive up from the distant valleys of the lower Rio Grande drainage, on both sides of the Mexican border. It had lazed here on the Canadian for months without disturbance, awaiting the return of those who had put it together, and it was in no mood to give up this good life for the alkaline dust of the *llanos* again. So their work was cut out for them.

Watching Abelardo and the *vaqueros,* Stanton thought the Mora horses, like his own, were just not accustomed to these formidably long-horned, rangy, incredibly quick and agile wild ones in contrast to their own stock, grown sleek and placid on the rich graze and plentiful water of the home high country. As a result, they responded too warily and indecisively, putting an additional burden on their exasperated riders. The truth was, he supposed, that the fault was his. He had just cut it too thin, attempting too much with too few. But the cattle were now in their possession, and however long the way to go, they had to make do.

They still had Heggie Duncan and his disarmed and dismounted herders in view in the cattle camp across the river behind them when Stanton roped a big, dappled Texas stallion among the horses he had commandeered and transferred his saddle to its back. The difference was immediately apparent. The big horse went right to work. He meant business and the longhorns knew it, giving way wherever he forced them.

Stanton rode swiftly up to where Abelardo was working the flank and ineffectually shouting himself hoarse.

"If we can keep them lined out and pushed hard enough for a few hours, they ought to settle down," he yelled to the Mora *segundo*. "They'll get the idea pretty quick. Try putting your men on the rest of those Texas horses. If this one's any example, they work these long-horned bastards a hell of a lot better than ours."

Abelardo nodded and doubled back. In quick rotation, he and his *vaqueros* transferred their rigs to their pick of the commandeered horses. The improvement was immediate. Even without Amelio's wagon, still up ahead of them, to fill in as drag, the cattle began to line out again in some kind of order.

From somewhere in the herd a big, piebald red steer which Stanton thought to be a full ten years old began to work its way up through the press toward the point. Its enormous spread of horns dominated any others Stanton could see. In less than a mile the big red shouldered its way out to the fore and took up a singleton lead, forcing the others to nose its tail or take the consequences. There were no challengers.

Others began to percolate to fixed positions in the moving herd, some dropping back and others pressing forward, as though in accord with some predetermined pecking order. Stanton had not noted this before among cattle and it interested him.

They overtook the wagon at the permanent camp of the *pastores*, where Amelio waited for them with their own cavvy of extra horses. Stanton knew the wolf of Mora and his *vaqueros* would have been content to night there, since the sun was already low enough to justify a halt. However, now that they had the herd in motion, he thought it wisest to continue on and work more fatigue into them, putting them further from the familiar bedding ground they had left on the river in the hope they would be less restless when they did stop and less fractious in the morning, when it was time to resume.

They passed through the *pastore* camp, waving to the women there who came shyly out to watch them string by, laboring up the talus slope of the ravine wall onto the great level of the open *llanos* beyond. The sun was gone and full darkness almost upon them when they came to first water on their backtrail. Stanton put the big stallion to the shoulder of the piebald red steer. The rangy, great-horned beast turned docilely enough, doubling back with a few others of the front ranks against those behind sufficiently to bring them to a halt. They milled a little, lowing protest at the broken pattern, then began to water and claim bedding room.

Amelio kindled a fire with faggots from the tarp beneath the wagon and set up his kitchen by the simple expedient of lowering the endgate Stanton had rigged to form a horizontal working surface. Abelardo named a pair of his *vaqueros* as first-shift nighthawks, then saddled a fresh horse and rode off, back the way they had come. Stanton saw that he took their saddle glass with him. He wanted to talk to the man, but it could wait.

The others had long since eaten and turned in when the wolf of Mora returned. Stanton, doing duty for Amelio, who had also turned in, served them both plates as Abelardo came up to the fire.

"I waited for you," Stanton said. "A long ride on top of a full day."

Abelardo grinned sheepishly.

"I didn't ask, *señor*, because I knew you would say it was not necessary. But I couldn't sleep until I was sure."

"Well?"

"They are still in their camp at the ford of the river."

"Then I would have been right, wouldn't I?"

181

"*Sí*. But they were angry. We left them afoot, but we did not come far. They could walk to here before morning and catch us in our blankets. I had to be sure they wouldn't try."

"They didn't."

Abelardo shook his head.

"I'd have met them on their way, if that's what they intended."

"Pride, 'Lardo. That's a very proud man back there. His kind usually are."

"*Sí. El es un escocés*. Fierce fighters, too."

"And sharp. What they call canny. A Scot's real talent. He won't forget what we did today. Or forgive. But he won't come after these cattle. Simply because if he did, he couldn't get back anything but what he had to start with. That won't be enough for him, now.

"He was going to drive the herd back to the settlements. I'm driving them west, toward the mountains. That'll tell him I believe they'll be worth more in the long run there than on east somewhere. He doesn't know why I believe that and he'll want to find out. So he'll give me time to show him. All the time necessary.

"When he's learned enough to know, he'll come for what he believes by right is his. He'll take it if he can, then. More, if he's let. He'll come when he thinks he's strong enough to clean the board, and he'll believe that's his right, too."

Abelardo blinked in surprise.

"You mean the cattle and horses you already have, too?"

"I mean the Corona, lock, stock, and barrel. That's why I'm telling you this. I want you to make Don Felipe understand I believe that's what's coming. Sooner or later. So he and the other Spanish and Mexican land-grant *rancheros* can be on guard, too."

"But the rancho is yours! You and the *señora* have papers of title, clear back to a Spanish king. And for these cattle, too. Signed by His Excellency himself."

"What I'm trying to tell you is that I am afraid before too long the signature of a Mexican governor won't be worth the paper it's written on. For a time, at least. I want you to get that across to Don Felipe. If Heggie Duncan may make a try for the Corona, I'm afraid others may make a try for Mora and some of the other ranchos."

"*Castígame santos!*" Abelardo protested angrily. "How do I tell the old *patrón* that and make him believe? Land his family has lived on for more than two hundred years, taken from him? Not while I live, *señor!* What kind of men are these *cabrones,* these *yanqui bandidos?*"

"No, don't get them wrong," Stanton corrected. "That's a serious mistake. Not bandits or ruffians. Not like the Cagles and others you've had to deal with, 'Lardo. They'll be strong men, like Heggie Duncan. They'll call themselves honest and believe they're right, or at least that they have the right to do what they intend."

"*Válgame Dios,* what kind of right is that?"

"They're a special breed of men. Much like

your own *conquistadores,* I should think. They see themselves as builders. In a way, I'm actually one of them, I suppose. Texas knows them. We will, too. Always before they've had free land ahead of them. Open, unused land, to be had by driving a stake or pitching a camp or clearing a patch or turning a milk cow out to graze. They're convinced of a pre-emptive right to put what they claim to better use. They believe it's their due and the will of God and will stand against any to defend it."

"I don't know about such things," Abelardo said stubbornly. "Only that in New Mexico a thief is still a thief."

"Don't count on it," Stanton said wryly. "Just get this through to Felipe Peralta. There's only one way to stop them. Strength and a hardness to match their own. That they respect. That they understand. Show them that and they'll accept you as one of them. They'll accept the stand you take. You saw proof of that, back on the river to-day. Fail and they'll plow you under just as surely as many of them already have the sod."

Abelardo drank off a fresh tin mug of steaming coffee and showed his big, white teeth.

"Tell me, *señor* Stanton," he said, "that one with the red beard today. What would you have done if he had not obeyed you?"

"I would have killed him."

"Or he would have killed you?"

"He'd have died with me."

"Yes. We would have seen to that," Felipe

184

Peralta's *segundo* agreed. "I think it will be that way at Mora, too. I will tell the *patrón* what you have said. But I make you a promise. There will be no plow on Don Felipe's rancho. I am Abelardo. They call me the wolf. We shall see. *Verdaderamente!*"

When they broke camp in gray light and hoorawed the herd up from its bedding-ground, the big red steer moved again to the fore and resumed the lead. Stanton watched with interest as others worked their way to the same relative positions they had picked the day before. Some took one flank, some the other. Some preferred the vanguard. Others were content to trail clear back in the dust at the drag.

There was no pattern to this positioning that Stanton could discover or any logic that he could apply. Not all of the animals seemed to exercise this characteristic, but enough did to make the whole herd much more cohesive and manageable than it had been initially. They all were grateful for the improvement, but even then it took endless riding back and forth, often at exasperated sprint, to keep the drive bunched and moving steadily without individuals spooking off in high-tailed protest or snatching perversely at tempting grass.

He kept Abelardo and the *vaqueros* pushing hard, putting the miles underfoot as fast as possible to work off the piss and vinegar and to break the most recalcitrant to the trail. He found that even the best of their horses winded after a couple of hours, particularly those working point and flank on both sides, and he ordered saddle stock rotated at that interval.

As a result, each man had ridden through six or seven mounts before arrival at night water put an end to the long day and Amelio built his supper fire. Stanton was grateful for the additional horses he had commandeered from Heggie Duncan and his Texans as a defensive measure.

They drove equally as hard the second day, making good another twenty-five or thirty miles. The cattle were noticeably quieter in bedding down and Stanton believed he had accomplished his purpose. In the morning he let the big red steer set its own pace.

This eased the labor, but it was still brutal work for so few men. He realized that at least two more hands would have been extremely useful and four not too many to efficiently manage a drive of any size. He filed this conclusion away with the others he was accumulating.

They moved steadily farther out onto the great flat of the *llanos* and gratefully picked up a stretch of their carefully prestaked backtrail. The dusty hours wore away monotonously. They hit next water on schedule, just short of sunset, and the *vaqueros* unsaddled wearily.

Stanton judged the red steer had taken them about twelve miles for the day, which seemed a fair average under normal conditions. It was slow, but he was content. Figuring wages for an augmented crew, food, and wear and tear, he could move beef, even in this inhospitable country, at a cost of a few cents less than a dollar a mile for an entire herd.

At that rate, a drive of seven or eight hundred miles was economically feasible if the herd of marketable beef was big enough. He doubted if anyone had ever had opportunity to make such a calculation under actual conditions such as these before, and he also filed this result away against later need.

While waiting for Amelio's amusingly formal bellow of *"La comida está servida!"* Stanton rode slowly out through the grazing cattle. There was some quarrelsome restlessness and humping. Part of their trials underway were due to the fact that Mexicans who had formerly owned most of this herd apparently did not castrate their animals as frequently as northern stockmen did.

He did not know if this was because of characteristic avoidance of additional labor, a humanitarian sensitivity, or some element of mother faith. At any rate, the herd was a melange of calves, weaners, cows, heifers, and big-balled bulls, each with their own notions of individual rights and privileges. He doubted if more than a quarter were more manageable gelded steers, which would be the sole component of a market herd.

He remembered his experience in bringing his first little bunch of river-bottoms beef out into the high country over the dry *jornada* of the

187

Santa Fe Trail and the losses he had suffered, enroute. He watched carefully for any sign of gaunting. Particularly among such steers as he could find, since they would be his prime interest in times to come.

Despite their dusty weariness, the stock seemed in fine shape. Especially the steers. He thought that under certain conditions and at a little slower daily pace, it might be possible to even continue to fatten them on a drive. At least on this grass. He was smiling broadly as he rode back into camp at Amelio's supper call.

The wiry *llanos* grass continued to soften and improve. Water became more frequent and sweeter. The distant blue mountains rose slowly above the western rim of the great, gently tilted plain. They saw their first antelope at a distance and used the last of their reclaimed stakes for firewood. More was to be had where there was water, now.

They crossed the wide trough of the Santa Fe Trail just below the big campground at Taylor Springs and nighted on the upper Canadian, almost at the head of its long swing north, with both the cone of Fire Mountain and the vast barrier of The Reef in view. In mid-morning, with the snow on the mountains looming clear and ever higher, a lone horseman appeared, racing across the Corona grass toward them.

With the glass Stanton recognized Helga Cagle. This puzzled him, but he saw with relief that although she was recklessly riding to the limit of her horse, it was not out of urgency but the sheer, excited devilment of the wind in her face and flying hair and pleasure at their return. He spurred up and rode out to meet her.

CHAPTER FIFTEEN

Stanton dipped into a shallow swale in the grass which took him temporarily from the view of the drive strung out behind him. The Cagle girl reached him there, pulling up at a little distance to dismount and run eagerly toward him. She moved with an unimpeded, free-swinging stride, as a boy did, but she would never be mistaken for one. The change in her was astounding.

She was dressed as 'Mana did for the saddle, in an outfit of 'Mana's making. Her hair was brushed out in a lustrous, free-flying golden cascade. Her lithe, long-legged body, gaunted before by hardship, had filled out firmly in splendid complement to her high, full breasts. Her magnificent eyes were alive with excitement. And her face, which he had remembered as rather plain in repose, was radiant. No vestige remained of the abused drab he had found in the malpais. He stepped down as she ran up.

"Oh, Spence," she cried, "I'm so glad you're back! I've been out here every day. It seems like for weeks."

Even her voice was different. It was low and vibrant, without a trace of the strident, nasal trans-Missouri twang Stanton remembered. He realized it cost her effort, for the words came more rounded and little slower than was natural, but the total effect was a complete change of personality. And that was not all.

Before he realized what was coming, she flung her arm about his neck, pulling up on tiptoe to kiss him. For a moment her mouth was warm and moist and searching against his. He was acutely conscious of her young body pressed hard against him. It moved as her mouth did and her breath quickened as she poured her bounty into him.

For that moment, Stanton was shaken to the soles of his boots and the grass underfoot was compellingly inviting. Then he gripped her shoulders and pushed her gently from him. She stepped quickly back, her breasts rising and falling rapidly, deep color flooding up from them to the roots of her hair. Her eyes rose slowly to meet his.

"Good God," she whispered hoarsely, "I didn't mean to do that!"

But her eyes betrayed her. The animal hunger and utter surrender were still there. He thought of 'Mana's pregnancy and a Southern custom as old as his Virginia birthplace, by which a master took a household wench at the same time as his lady to provide a wet nurse for the expected child of the house when the time came. He knew that he could take this one. Here and now or at any other time that suited his fancy. And as often. In spite of her admiration for 'Mana, even the love and devotion she felt for her benefactress. Because she loved him more and wanted him. Or believed she did.

"I'm sorry," she continued softly. "I'm just so excited that I kind of got carried away."

Stanton smiled at her. "Forget it," he said. "It doesn't hurt a man to know he's welcome home. That's how I got the message."

She hung her head meekly.

"That's how it was meant," she said in a small voice. "Welcome home, Mr. Stanton."

He took her arm and walked her to her horse. Giving her a hand up, he stepped to his own saddle and kicked his horse into a lope. Helga kicked up with him and they rode on toward the mountains.

When the headquarters came into view, Stanton was surprised. His own labors and those of Amelio and Abelardo and the Mora *vaqueros* were fresh in his mind and weary in his bones, but those at home had not been idle, either. Jaime had done well with the responsibilities with which he had been left.

There was no longer any cut stone from the quarry stacked in the yard. It had been mortared up a full two stories on the foundation lines Stanton had drawn and ridge, roof, and floor beams had been square-hewed and set so that the enclosure and framing of another dream had materialized. It was far from the eventual great house he had envisioned for 'Mana, but the new addition contributed a satisfactory hint of the grandeur yet to come.

He also saw that several more small adobes had been squared off down by the corrals and were rising from their own sod, adding to the makings of a small village there, and he was well pleased. Helga reined closer to him as he slowed momentarily to relish the growing silhouette against the mountains towering beyond.

"That's why I've been riding out toward the Trail every day," she said. "Everybody else was busy and I had to do something. Jaime said he could spare me easiest."

Stanton noted that in the first flush of her extraordinary welcome she had used his first name but had twice since reverted to the formal "Mr." He appreciated the effort and thought that in spite of what she had betrayed in that first moment, she might not after all be the problem he feared she could be. He found the thought reassuring. Nodding at her explanation, he drew his gun.

"Let's let them know we're coming in."

He fired two quick shots into the air and kicked his horse up again.

The home people were all in the yard when they rode in. Jaime and Raul Archuleta and Benny and Ramón. Mama Archuleta and her younger children. Two or three brown, weathered male faces Stanton did not recognize. And 'Mana, alone on the veranda, for all her eagerness waiting proudly, as the *patrona* should, on

193

the threshold of her house, for him to come to her.

He did, and took her in his arms and kissed her, then turned with equal pride, pointing out eastward toward the undulating grass where the point of two thousand head of Texas cattle was just plodding into view. No words were equal to that gesture.

Jaime cut loose with a shrill Missouri yell and vaulted onto the horse Stanton had just ridden in. Papa Archuleta and his two older sons ran for their own horses behind the house. Someone else leaped onto Helga's mount. All rode breakneck after Jaime, excitedly yipping their way to the cattle. Helga watched them go, then quietly entered the house and disappeared.

Spencer Stanton stood motionless on his veranda with his arm about his wife, aware with wonder of the already slight thickening of her body, filling out the hollows above her hips. They stood there a long time, not speaking and with no need to do so, until Jaime and Abelardo and the big, piebald red steer led the herd in.

Jaime chose the way, bringing the longhorns right through the yard, proudly passing the thick, dusty snake of lowing, living flesh before the veranda like a conquering host passing in review. It was a sight to be long remembered. Stanton relished it to the full. 'Mana had promised him a son; he had promised her a ranch. They were a kind to keep their promises.

When Amelio waved in passing from the seat of the wagon in the dust of the drag, they turned, Stanton's arm about 'Mana's shoulders, to enter the house. Helga Cagle stood in the doorway. Stanton did not know for how long. She stepped aside. As he passed, Stanton put his free arm about her, as well, taking her with them on into the big, flagstoned living room.

She glanced quickly and uneasily at him. He smiled at her reassuringly. So did 'Mana.

"Helga's been a wonderful help to me, Spence," she said. "In fact, she's become absolutely indispensable. We've already picked out her room in the new wing."

"If it's all right with you for me to stay," the girl said with sharp apprehension to Stanton.

"You ought to know by now who's boss in this house," he told her, and he gave them both a little tug of a hug before he dropped his arms from their shoulders.

Helga went into the kitchen corner and bustled there, shaking down the grate of the stove and lifting the lids to refuel the fire. 'Mana led Stanton across to one of the big chairs and knelt before him to pull off his boots, a luxury of wifely service he had permitted himself since they first had a fireplace. Mostly because this little personal end of the day ritual seemed to please 'Mana.

"Jaime and I hired two new hands," she said. "From Taos. Jaime went to Father Frederico and he found them for us. Carpenters and good cabinetmakers. For the house. Both can work stock, too, and will if there's need, later."

"Good," Stanton said. "There'll be need. And not as much later as you think. Two thousand head of longhorns is one hell of a lot of cattle. Abelardo and I found that out between the breaks of the *llanos* and here."

"One thing, Spence. They're family men. According to the old custom, here. Their wives and children will be over the mountains before first snow."

"And welcome. If the Corona's home to us, why shouldn't it be to all our people?"

"Maybe easier said than done. The women and the little ones will look to you as *patrón,* too. Their troubles will be yours."

"You said that's the way it's always been."

"So long as you know what you're letting yourself in for. We've had to start some new adobes for them."

"So I saw."

"We settled on four, for now. In case we find we need more help in the spring."

"We will. Before then. Some of this stock has been running wild for years. A lot of it has never even been branded. And quite a bunch has to be culled out as we can get to it. There'll be no shortage of work. You and Jaime have done wonders while I was gone. No trouble?"

"Plenty!" 'Mana said, and sat herself on Stanton's lap. "I can't keep a breakfast down. Helga won't let me even poke my head out until

196

Jaime and the boys have finished and she's cleared and washed the dishes. It's the cooking smells, she says. Anyway, you'll have to get used to it, I'm afraid."

"Nothing to it," he told her with a grin. "It'll only last a few more weeks. Goes away when you get bigger and begin to waddle like a duck. Take my word for it. I'm an old hand."

"We'll see. There are some things you can't do anything about, whatever you think, *señor ranchero*. Baby making's one. Why don't you try bragging on what you know something about and tell me just what kind of a cattle thief you turned out to be?"

"No problem. Must be a hidden talent, I guess. Not a hitch. Not a shot fired. Not even any loud talk. Just a simple agreement between gentlemen."

"You're not only a thief, you're a liar!" 'Mana said severely, then kissed him. "I'm so relieved there was no serious trouble. I could tell by your face as you came in. Like a boy with a string of fish he's caught all by himself. These have been anxious weeks for me. So we have the cattle. But it's not over — it's not done yet, is it?"

"We're home and the beef's on our grass."

"That isn't what I mean. The right and wrong of it — that hasn't been settled —"

"Well, to tell you the truth, there just may be a big, red Scot come by one day with a trifling complaint or two."

"That's what I was afraid of. What is that herd

actually going to cost us, then, Spence? When the whole bill is in and we have to pay?"

Stanton recognized her earnestness and dropped his banter.

"I don't know," he answered, as honestly as he knew how. "But no more than they're worth. I promise you that."

"We're within the law?"

"Our law, yes. Mexican law. God's, if you like. But there's no telling, now, how long that will last."

"Spence, I told you my fears. I sent you to Santa Fe because of them. Now, you tell me yours. We've had the war with Texas, and we lost. Twice, in fact. Two wars. Do you think we will have another — with the States, this time?"

"I'm almost sure, *querida*," Stanton admitted reluctantly. "Not soon, I don't think. But sometime. It's inevitable, I'm afraid."

'Mana sighed, deeply and sadly.

"I have the same feeling. And to think that when it comes, I will be married to the enemy."

Stanton tried to lighten her mood as well as his own. In this warm and exciting hour of triumphant homecoming, with this russet golden woman in his arms after weeks of separation, Washington-on-the-Brazos and Washington-on-the-Potomac and Mexico City were far away and inconsequential places. He squeezed 'Mana and answered her with a contented chuckle.

"Or I will. Point of view. And there's no help

198

for it, now. Maybe you went to bed with the wrong man, after all."

"No. Not ever. It's just that I'm happy and in love and want nothing changed." She put her hand on the firm round of her belly. "Doubly so, now."

The door across the big room opened and Helga Cagle went out into the yard with the Indian wood basket from the kitchen. 'Mana stirred guiltily and pushed herself up from his lap.

"See what a bad influence you are? It's time to help her start supper."

Stanton clung to a hand.

"She's a big girl, now," he protested.

"So you've noticed, have you?" 'Mana asked wickedly. "And only a month of sleeping alone!" She laughed at him and continued, "She's learning fast, but I don't know for the life of me how the poor dear ever put a pound on her body with what she knew about civilized cooking. Don Felipe's hogs live better. Go look at the farm and see if you can find something for the lord and master to criticize."

She went across to the kitchen. Stanton pulled on his boots and hat and let himself out. Going around to a solidly framed doorway in the new red stone of the addition, he stepped within. The new structure appeared grander than had the plans on paper. He thought that the labor and handwork of erection lent the wood and stone an aura of proportion and dignity and permanence which could not be envisioned in the mind's eye, alone.

The two new men were laying the floor of the upper hall on the heavy beams above. He climbed a ladder to them and learned they were Diego Fernandez and Luís Dominguín. They were solid, settled men and obviously knew their trade well. The planks they were setting and pegging down were of mountain spruce, whip-sawed and hand-finished to uniform width and thickness. Laid edge-grain-up in strips two inches wide and a good four deep, they created a beautifully grained pattern with the variegated warm coloring of the natural wood itself, and formed a smooth, polished floor as solid and impervious to time and wear as the thick stone of the walls.

He complimented Diego and Luís on their skill and care and stepped through a framed partition to the opening of an upper window. The woodpile was directly below. Jaime was standing beside the chopping block, talking earnestly with Helga Cagle. Their voices were indistinct, but Stanton thought there might be a minor disagreement of some kind between them. The girl appeared calm enough, but Jaime seemed a little more testy than was his usual nature. Wanting to talk to the Missourian himself, Stanton returned to the ladder and descended to ground level again.

Rounding a corner of the addition, he almost collided with Helga, returning to the kitchen with her laden wood basket.

"Want me to carry that on in for you?" he asked.

She refused.

"No, thanks, Mr. Stanton. I can manage fine."

But the smile she gave him was so blinding as to be ample reward for the common courtesy of the offer. He watched her go on and disappear around the next turn of the new walls, her body swinging rhythmically and the basket of wood no burden at all. When he turned to resume, Jaime was facing him, his eyes murky and an unaccustomed scowl on his face.

Stanton remembered the scene he had witnessed from above. He looked after the Cagle girl again and grinned at his *segundo*.

"What the hell," he demanded, "you turning stud on me?"

"None of your damned business!" Jaime snapped.

Startled but in no way offended, Stanton shrugged good-naturedly.

"All right," he agreed. "Let's talk cattle, then. That sure as the devil is."

Jaime made a visible effort and his touchy mood seemed to pass.

"Sure, Spence. I'm sorry. That's what I came up to tell you. I had them throw the longhorns in on Two Mile Bottom, with that big arroyo between them and the rest. For the time being."

"Good," Stanton told him. "Come on in and

have a drink. Lord knows you've earned it."

To his surprise, the Missourian declined.

"Thanks, but I better get back down and redd up our adobe, now that Amelio's back, before he starts raising holy hell over my housekeeping."

Turning, he walked quickly away.

CHAPTER SIXTEEN

Days blended swiftly and indistinguishably together. 'Mana's morning sickness passed as she
thickened. Aspen stands mottling the evergreen
slopes of the lower mountains turned red and
gold and yellow as night cold crept down from the
vestigial ice and snow still cresting the highest
peaks.

Stanton farmed his cattle as assiduously as a
man of the plow did his fields. Individually, animal by animal, as fast as each could be gotten to.
It was endless and grueling work and time ran
constantly against them. Each animal was graded
by age and kind and condition and quality and
separated into like groups. Each group was hazed
onto its own area of graze, apart from others.

Some were intermingled, where it seemed likely
a desirable cross might result. There were about
fifty of the older steers and cow mothers which
were judged too far past prime for one reason or
another. These were marked apart for table use
at the main house and the adobes and for
Chato's people, whenever the Utes came down
from the mountains. No waste was allowed and
not yet could the Corona afford the best beef for
its own use.

All others were branded. Any marks of previous ownership were vented when the Corona crown was burned through the hair. Those to be desexed were castrated and mountain oysters were added to the table fare.

A reliable inventory gradually emerged. Even after culling, the total count finally rose to slightly more than three thousand head. More than enough to insure a good rate of increase, even when a substantial seasonal sell-off became possible. Of that number, nearly five hundred head were marketable, drivable steers, at or coming up to prime.

Successfully delivered to any shipping point along the Missouri, they alone were worth more in cash on the hoof than Stanton had paid for the entire combined herd. And he knew, now, that when the time came, he could get them to the river. His experience on the *llanos* convinced him of that. He saw to it that the big piebald red longhorn was well taken care of against that day. Before the end of another season — two at most — he was determined that Corona beef would be on the move.

Always, in the dawn and the heat of day and the dusk of sunset, he kept a wary eye to the north and east for the big, red-bearded man he knew would come. But the only arrival from the States was a big tandem freight rig which came in from the Santa Fe Trail at Taylor Springs with the balance of the order he had placed through Sol Wetzel.

He talked privately with the freighters and learned that the annexation of Texas had become a fact. It had passed Congress by joint resolution and had been ratified by the Texas Republic. Formal announcement and implementation was expected early in the year. Stanton checked dates as the freighters believed them to be and realized that when he had faced Heggie Duncan on the banks of the Canadian, the canny Scot had already known of these events, and he thought he understood now what Duncan was waiting for.

There was much excitement as the freight wagons were unloaded. Furnishings and linens and all manner of things which he and Wetzel had believed necessary to a new mother and the coming of an heir to the Corona. 'Mana hoorawed him considerably over his prodigality with these last items.

There were also tools and hardware and window glass, and the new wing of the house came along steadily after their arrival. When it was roofed and tiled and glazed, Stanton put the stock crew to helping at the adobes when he could, so that they were finished at about the same time.

'Mana sent word to Father Frederico and he came over the mountains from Taos to bless the new structures. The women and families of Diego and Luís made the crossing with him, bringing such possessions as they did not wish to leave behind. It was obviously a permanent move. They also brought with them two younger men of one of their clans for whom the *padre* vouched as able *vaqueros*. Stanton found them welcome. He armed them and gave them their choice of the horses in the corrals.

The ceremonies of invoking God's blessing teetered between solemnity and fiesta. But the intent was simple and sincere. All took part. Stanton found himself standing at the fore, as was expected of the *patrón*. To his surprise, it gave him a curious feeling of fulfillment and content.

Afterward there was a pit-roasted quarter of beef and much *aguardiente*. At 'Mana's invitation, crew and families danced on the flagstone floor of the living room of the main house, more spacious now because the kitchen corner and the big trestled supper table had been moved to rooms provided for them on the ground floor of the new wing.

'Mana and Stanton went to bed while the *fandango* music still played, occupying for the first time the large sitting-room and bedroom suite he had designed for them on the upper floor, across the hall from the now well-furnished if unoccupied nursery. In the morning, Father Frederico started on his long ride back to Taos, promising to return over the mountains to be present for 'Mana's delivery.

Snows came. Light falls in this favored place, through which stock, like the wild game, readily pawed for the abundant cured grass still on the stem beneath. The coats of the cattle began to shag up, but they continued to put on weight.

There was time, now, to cut aspen poles while the sap was down and sled them from the mountains. With these they built a long, sod-roofed shed along the north side of one of the corrals, open to the kindlier exposure of the south, where the horses of the working cavvy, held for day to day use, could take shelter and feed when it stormed or an infrequent norther blew. And a lean-to was added to the tool and tack shed to shelter the chuckwagon Stanton had devised.

'Mana grew heavier and more radiantly beautiful, but she seemed to turn more to herself and what was growing within. She spent increasing hours before the fire in her upper sitting room or puttering in the nursery, going over the things Stanton had ordered out from the River. He in his turn grew daily more aware of this natural withdrawal and in spite of himself grew restless because of it.

He would have turned instinctively to Jaime as a substitute with whom to talk and pass idle time, but although Stanton could detect no change in their relationship or cause for it, the Missourian remained even more remote than 'Mana. Jaime worked prodigiously as long as there was light and came up to the main house only when necessity demanded. Stanton was concerned but could get no satisfaction from him.

When Helga moved into her new quarters behind the kitchen and Jaime's old room again became available, he declined to return to the house, claiming it was better management for him to be near the crewmen and associate with them. Stanton might have bought this as good judgement, but the Missourian did not do this either, falling into his bed in Amelio's adobe as soon as he had eaten.

Stanton made the unclaimed room over into the ranch office and busied himself there as often as possible, but found little satisfaction in it. The long evenings were interminable and the living room too big and empty to face alone.

Helga learned to make biscuits and bread and pies and to roast even the toughest cuts of meat to succulent tenderness. She took over the whole of the kitchen chores, disdaining any help from Amelio or any of the women at the adobes. Her new, self-chosen personality continued to develop with seldom a slip. With each passing day she spoke more as 'Mana did and began to rapidly pick up Spanish as well. Stanton noted that she looked often at him as she worked, but her devotion was wholly to 'Mana and she was on the stairs a thousand times a day on voluntary, thoughtful little errands for the *patrona*'s comfort.

She allowed herself only one pleasure. She loved to ride and except in storm somehow found time in her long and busy day to spend an hour or so in the saddle. Stanton frequently encountered her out on the range. Too frequently to suppose it was wholly by accident. And always when he was alone. She would appear suddenly from some draw or down the slope of some ridge, hair flying, graceful, aglow with the joy of living. Reining up, she would ride alongside him, whatever his destination or chore.

She was interested in any task at hand and he found her easy to talk to, out there like that. As a consequence, he told her much and she began to learn a little about beef cattle in this country and how Spencer Stanton believed they should be managed and handled. It was a pleasant, un-studied companionship and he came to welcome it, regretting the swift passage of the time she had alotted herself.

He told 'Mana of these meetings, early on. She smiled approvingly.

"She needs encouragement, Spence," she said. "All she can get. She has so much to learn. She's working very hard, trying to make herself over into something she wasn't when she came here. That's hard to do. Especially when you don't know how in the first place. You should help her all you can. She looks to you, you know. We all should help her. She's earned that much, believe me."

So Helga rode with him regularly, three or four times a week. And continued to do so for three or four months. Then, as suddenly as they had begun, and with no more explanation, these meetings stopped. If she continued to saddle up, she rode elsewhere. Stanton didn't ask, but he found he missed the pleasure of her company. He wondered at the abrupt breaking of the pleasant pattern he had come to anticipate as he wondered at Jaime's inexplicable withdrawal, but he did not get his answer for nearly a week.

It was a windy night beyond the panes of the undraped windows but snug within. Stanton was sitting before an ebbing fire in the office fireplace. He had been reading in Spanish a *Memorial de Alonso de Benevides*, an historic account of that early friar's explorations and travels in that part of New Spain which he called Cibola, which he had picked up in Santa Fe, and he had trimmed the lamp down low to rest his eyes.

It was late. The kitchen was long since dark and the house silent. He was half dozing in reverie, reluctant to face the cold bedroom above and the chill linen of the cot upon which he had been sleeping while 'Mana's time drew closer.

Quietly, without a knock, the office door swung gently open and Helga slipped in, pressing it closed with her back. The latch clicked loudly in the silence and she stood there, still leaning back against the door, looking across the room at him.

Her hair had been loosed from the knot in which she normally wore it during the day. It hung down nearly to her waist. She wore a long wrapper and soft, silent moccasins were on her feet. Stanton was startled and sat up abruptly, fearing something might be amiss upstairs.

"What is it?" he asked sharply. "Something wrong?"

She shook her head.

"Sssh!" she warned softly. "No need to wake the house. I couldn't sleep and I knew you were still down here with a fire. Is it all right?"

Relieved, he eased back and indicated the fireplace.

"Sure. Help yourself."

She passed his deep chair and turned before the fire to face him, hiking the rear hem of her wrapper to let the glowing heat at the backs of her knees without exposure in front. She rocked on her feet in a movement of pleasure which seemed to ripple through her body.

"Mmm!" she breathed. "Feels good. It's cozy in here."

Stanton nodded, waiting, knowing something was on her mind. She smiled and took her time, seeming to relish it, but he could see a troubled uncertainty far back in her eyes. After a moment she spoke hesitantly.

"Know why I haven't ridden out to find you the last few days?"

"No, but I wondered some," Stanton admitted.

"Because it just wasn't getting through to you why I was doing it in the first place. All these weeks. I tried to tell you once."

Stanton's brow knit.

"I don't think I understand, Helga," he lied, trying to forestall what he feared was coming.

But once she was started, her uncertainty fled.

"God, isn't it plain enough?" she whispered. "I love you, Spence Stanton. You hear that? You're making me say it. I want you. Even for a little while. Just once, even. To remember."

Stanton had no answer he could trust and made none, letting his eyes lift significantly toward the ceiling in the direction of the upper bedroom in the other wing. The girl dropped the hem of her wrapper and her hands clenched into tight little fists of anguish.

"Don't tell me about her!" she protested intensely. "I know all that. I've fought myself to hell and gone for months over it. I know what I owe her, how much I respect her — yes, love her too, I guess, when it comes to that. You don't know how much. You can't."

"I know how much I love her," Stanton said quietly. "I thought I made that clear to you the day you met us with the longhorns."

"Oh Christ, try to understand, please!" Helga begged. "I don't know how to do this. I don't even know the right words. It took everything I had to come in here like this. I wouldn't do anything to hurt her. I never will, as long as I live. Believe me. I'd die before I let her know. Ever. But I've got to think of me a little, too. And I keep thinking of you, sleeping alone up there on that cot. All these weeks. All these cold nights. You could do so much for me. I could do so much for you. And no harm to anyone. Just so I could know you'd loved me. Even just once."

Slowly, sadly, Stanton shook his head.

"I promise it'll end the day she has her baby," Helga pleaded desperately. "When you have her back, it'll be like it never happened. If you don't believe me, you can send me away, then. Anything. I don't care. Just about now. Just until then. Please!"

Stanton gripped hard at rationality and forced himself to speak with paternal firmness.

"That kind of thing never works out, girl. I'm a hell of a lot older than you are and I know. It just never happens that way, no matter how two people intend it. It winds up exactly what it is, with nothing wonderful or beautiful about it."

"But it can be."

"No. Instead of no harm to anyone, there's harm to everyone. Most of all to the other girl. The one you think you want to be. Whether it's her doing or not. She winds up with nothing, Helga. Not even her own pride and self-respect."

He came to his feet, suddenly needing the confidence of his height.

"You're all worked up and not thinking straight," he continued, easier, now. "You're believing a lot of things about yourself — and me — that just aren't true. Or even possible. I'll pour you a drink and you go back to bed. It'll all seem different in the morning and we can both forget tonight."

He crossed to a cabinet and took down a bottle and poured a generous half a tumbler for her, neat. She spoke to his back as he did so, her voice low and intense.

"I'm no child! Stop treating me like one."

"Stop behaving like one," he answered without turning.

"You think I'm bad," she continued, her speech quickening. "Jezebel. A slut. But I'm not. I swear it. I told you once I was good. Clean through. And that wasn't so easy, either. A lot of times. But God, I love you. And I'm going to have you. Because you're a man. That's something I learned the hard way. It's in you, whether you want it or not, and there isn't a damned thing any of you can do about that!"

He turned back with the tumbler and saw that she had loosed the tie of her wrapper and dropped the garment to the floor about her feet. She stood there magnificently naked in the warm glow of the low-trimmed lamp and the firelight. She was taut with emotion and her lip trembled pleadingly with shame and determination, begging for understanding and assent.

Stanton looked at her helplessly. She was so damned right that he was a man and the pair of yards which separated them was a very small space, indeed. It was an exceedingly difficult and dangerous moment. Then he indicated the discarded wrapper and the chair in which he had been reading.

"Get that back on and sit down," he said in a voice he couldn't quite steady. "I guess I'm going to have to tell you something —"

She stood there in silhouette against the fire, not moving, defiant, shame now turned to full-breasted pride in the effect she was having upon him.

"God damn it, get it on!" he repeated hoarsely. "Or I'll waken 'Mana and have her put you back to bed."

The defiance held for a moment then faded, and the shame flooded back. She snatched up the wrapper and drew it on, closing it to her chin, so that she was fully covered. Stepping from the hearth, she dropped into the chair. Her eyes turned up to him in the mute appeal of a child expecting discipline.

Stanton exhaled, suddenly limp with relief. He became aware of the forgotten tumbler in his hand and downed it in two quick, unbroken gulps. Setting the empty tumbler aside, he took her place on the hearth before the fire, looking down at her.

"That's better," he said, again in control of himself. "That was an unfair thing you did."

"I know," she whispered miserably. "I'm sorry. Ashamed. I'll never do it again. With anybody."

"Until the right time comes," he corrected. "Just be damned sure, next time. But you're entitled to know why it wouldn't work with me. Why it couldn't."

He picked up the tumbler again and went to the cabinet and refilled it while she waited silently.

"I was married once before," he said slowly, returning to the hearth. "In Virginia. A long time ago. We had a farm. A plantation, really, except our crop was stock instead of tobacco or cotton and we hired our hands instead of buying them. We had a big house and two young sons. Jimmy and Blair. Everything that a man could want. Or a woman, either, I thought."

He stopped, recalling the dark, proud recesses of memory of which only 'Mana knew the full story. He had not thought to share it with another, but the conviction persisted that it might be of value here.

Helga misunderstood his hesitancy and her curiosity outran her patience.

"What happened?"

"My wife did what you thought you wanted me to do, tonight. She took another man into my bed. A secret, you said. For a little while. No harm to anyone. Maybe that's the way she meant it to be, too. Maybe even just once, in the beginning. I don't know. I never did.

"But when the time came, she had to tell me the new child in her belly wasn't mine. Maybe she wanted to tell me. I've never known about that, either. And to protect herself, knowing everything was destroyed, she told me she wanted everything I had. My sons, my house, my property, my pride. Everything but my life.

"Because they were destroyed, I gave them to her — to them. They no longer had any value to me. And I went away. Because there was no going back. Even in memory. Not ever."

The girl's great eyes looked steadily up at him and he saw tears in them.

"You're lovely — and young, Helga," Stanton went on, doggedly determined that she should fully understand. "I'll never forget that vision of you standing here a few minutes ago where I'm standing now. Because I'm a man. I'll treasure it in my way. You have a great gift to give. But you can only give it once.

"Even then, even knowing that, even though I knew I'd be doing great harm to you, I might have taken it. God knows I wanted to. Don't doubt yourself as a woman about that. Ever."

He stopped and smiled at her.

"But, you see," he continued, "it would only have been a moment, a night, a few weeks. 'Mana is my life."

He saw that at last she understood.

"You're entitled to yours someday, too, honey."

Her head dropped. Suddenly she burst from the chair and ran from the room. Stanton turned the empty tumbler around and around in his hand. When he heard the distant sounds of the girl's door closing, far across the house, he flung the glass into the fireplace.

"Jesus Christ!" he breathed.

CHAPTER SEVENTEEN

Stanton was up early enough to need a lamp to come downstairs, but Helga was before him, the stove hot and his breakfast ready. Whatever it cost her, she answered his good morning with a smile and poured his coffee with a steady hand. He liked that. Others might call it resilience, the easy way out of a corner. Toughness was the word he preferred, the ability to face facts and make do. Without loss of spirit. It was worthy of the Corona. So, he thought, was she. He complimented her on the morning meat he wolfed and went without further comment out into the dawn cold.

Early on, Raul Archuleta had tried to see that one of his boys had the *patrón*'s horse saddled and in the yard when he stepped from the house. They all knew better than that, now. They minded their own starting chores and let him boot it down, high-heeled, to the corrals alone, his breath steaming in the air. They smiled as the women called to him from the warm doorways of the adobes.

"*Buenos días, señor. Buenos días, patrón.*"

"*Buenos días, mamasita. Buenos días, señora* Dominguín. The baby's croup better this morning?"

They let him swing his own saddle from the rack and spin a loop into his own rope. He dropped it over the big dappled stallion he had taken from Heggie Duncan and walked down the rope to the wildly snorting, farting beast with no helping hand offered. They understood, now. All of them. Personal service rendered him was a vanity. Service rendered the Corona was of benefit to all.

He asked for Jaime Henry and was told the Missourian had ridden out before light. Somewhere yonder. No one knew.

"For some geese, maybe," Amelio suggested without conviction. "He took the shotgun. I don't know what else for."

Neither did Stanton. He doubted the big migrators were sufficient sport for Jaime at this early hour of a working day. At this time of year they could be easily had with a pistol at any of the open seeps. And they weren't likely to be welcomed by Helga at the kitchen. They were too much trouble to scald and pluck when hanging beef was at hand unless there was a special need of down for pillows or quilting. Still, there was no accounting for Jaime's notions these days.

Stanton, with Diego and Luís, beat the sun onto the grass. The big red steer, with a certain perversity, and his long legs, had led a small bunch of shorter-coupled animals straight through a clay bog and some had picked up thirty pounds or more of cumbersome dewballs, caked to and painfully dangling from the hair of hindquarters and tails.

They had to be roped down, one by one, and this unwanted burden beaten off between two clubs. It was lively work, for the downed animals snorted and kicked wildly, hating the ropes and sure the blows were for them.

Raul Archuleta came by, driving a likely looking fresh cow and its bawling calf to join the little dairy bunch at the corrals. He reported he had met Jaime at the upper end of Two Mile Bottom and that the Missourian had told him that if the *patrón* wanted to see him, he could be found over there.

Stanton was puzzled. Even a little irritated. Ordinarily his *segundo* would have come on the run when he heard he was wanted. Maybe it was time to have this out in the open, too, and put an end to it. Leaving Diego and Luís to beat off the rest of the caked dewballs and manure from the bunch they were working, Stanton rode over the ridge.

Tracks were easy to follow in the hoarfrost yet clinging to the grass on the shaded slope. Leaving Raul Archuleta, Jaime had ridden down into the brush thickets along the seep which drained the bottom. Stanton followed him there. The Missourian's tracks doubled back on themselves on the edge of a small meadow deep in the thickets. As Stanton pulled up to unravel them, Jaime's voice snapped behind him with the flat, hard ring of a pistol shot.

"Hold it right there! Ease that belt careful and drop it."

Startled as much by the tone as the order, Stanton twisted in his saddle. Jaime stood a few yards away, without his usual belted gun but with a big, smoothbore scattergun loaded with God knows what braced across his hip. His face was thinned, pale, frozen hard, and he looked as if he had not slept. Blinking in astonishment, Stanton hesitated. The scattergun muzzle jerked warningly.

"You heard me, God damn it!" Jaime said sharply, his voice taut and thin.

Stanton unbuttoned his saddle coat and slipped the buckle and let his gunbelt slip to the ground.

"Hell of a way to say good morning!" he protested. "What the devil's the matter with you, anyway?"

"You'll find out," Jaime answered, backing up to set the shotgun aside and ripped off his own jacket. "Step down and peel out of the coat if you want a fair chance."

Stanton had not had this before. Not on the Corona. Never from Jaime. And he didn't like it, whatever the reason. He swung down, kicked his gunbelt out of the way, hung his coat on the saddlehorn, and started toward the Missourian.

"Just what have you got in mind, son?" he asked.

"Save your breath, you dirty son of a bitch!" Jaime rasped at him. "You're going to need it.

Because I'm going to beat the living shit out of you."

Jaime spun his hat away and came at him like a cougar at kill. Stanton set himself and swung. There was no time for anything else and his patience was short. He had the advantage of a full twenty pounds. It was all behind the blow. He meant it to end all of this damned foolishness, right now. But it failed to connect.

Jaime weaved aside without slackening and came in past it, feinting and then pistoning hard with each hand, in close with incredible speed. What was lacking in weight was counterbalanced by quickness and murderous accuracy. The first punch slanted up into the vee of Stanton's ribs, rocking him back onto his heels. The second rammed with a blinding flash of light flush against his jaw below the ear.

Stanton staggered but could not keep his feet under him and he went down hard onto the flat of his back. Shaking his head in an attempt to clear it, he raised unsteadily to his elbows. Jaime stood spraddle-legged above him, lips back from his teeth and blood on his knuckles, wavering menacingly in Stanton's dazed vision.

"For Christ's sake, Jaime!" he said thickly, protesting the senselessness of it.

His answer was a jolting kick in the ribs with the sharp toe of a Spanish boot.

"Get up, you bastard. You ain't seen nothing yet!"

Stanton shook his head to steady his vision

and make some head or tail to it all. The boot stabbed his ribs again, and that tore it. He grunted and grabbed the boot and rolled with it, flinging Jaime over him in an involuntary dive onto his face a dozen feet away. He heard the breath burst from the Missourian as he landed. By the time Jaime was up again and coming back, Stanton was onto his own feet, steadied by a surging flow of cold anger.

That was a prime lesson, learned long ago. Before Jaime Henry was born. A man who permitted his anger to heat beyond control was most often beaten at the outset. Heat clouded the mind — and let the reflexes run ungoverned. The cold man was the dangerous man. He had a great advantage. A raging fury was occasionally solace for the soul, but it was a luxury Spencer Stanton seldom permitted himself, even in such a reasonless thing as this. And never when the stakes were of any consequence.

It was a lesson Jaime seemed to understand as well. The hard, pinched whiteness was in him still. The fierce malevolence in his eyes. But he came in warily, bobbing, weaving, using his lightness and speed shrewdly. Stanton had always believed his own reflexes quicker than most. Deceptively so, for his weight and height. But he realized that this deadly serious, whang-leather young Missourian could dance him to death if he permitted it. So he deliberately coarsened his own tactics.

He swung as he had before, hard, telegraphing

a little, and barely glanced off Jaime's shoulder. He took two more hard ones to the ribs and the side of the head for it. He began to let his breath come harder, as though winded, and watched Jaime's tempo quicken eagerly.

He let it seem heavy-footed, but he shifted his balance as little as possible. In this way he kept in balance, well set to use his whole body when opportunity afforded. As he intended, Jaime misinterpreted this too.

The quick, jolting jabs darted in. Some he anticipated and turned aside. Some he did not, and they hurt. But he took them in trade and waited, thinking only that they were leaving marks which would have to be explained to 'Mana, and that would not be easy.

Even if she were here, now, 'Mana would not believe. Not with Jaime. To her, in a very special way, he was their son. But the poison had to be let out of him, whatever it was, and there was one thing he had yet to learn.

A short left clipped Stanton's jaw again, dropping him to one knee, and Jaime finally made his mistake. He surged in triumphantly to finish it and Stanton catapulted upward into him. Jaime tried to reverse and Stanton hit him as he hung on his toes. It was not one of the full, powerful swings he had come to expect but a short, straight drive with the combined weight of their oppositely moving bodies behind it. Jaime reeled back and down. Stanton leaped after him and as he started to get up, jerked him to his feet and hit him again.

Again Jaime went down, looking pained and surprised now, but he stubbornly rolled instinctively to his belly and pumped his knees under him to get up. Stanton grabbed the back of his collar, hauled him upright, spun him, and hit him again, full in the face.

The Missourian staggered back and slumped to the ground, supporting himself on his hands. Stanton stood over him, waiting. Jaime looked up at him, his mouth bloody, the same inexplicable venom in his eyes, and slowly shook his head in an unwilling and bitter admission of enough.

It was over, barely three minutes after Stanton had halted on taut command. Time enough to risk and maybe destroy a boy-man relationship which had grown to full man-to-man size and closeness. However helpless he was in the situation, however he had been from the start, Stanton felt a deep surge of regret.

He offered Jaime his hand. Jaime pointedly avoided it and clumsily and unsteadily got himself to his feet unaided. He stood there rocking a little, breathing deeply, glaring balefully. His battered lips moved with effort.

"God damn it, I tried," he said thickly, with almost a sob. "My friend. Spencer Stanton. The great *ranchero!*"

His scorn and bitterness were scathing.

"You rotten, horny old son of a bitch, you'd hump your own mother! Your own kid on the way, and doing what you been to 'Mana behind her back, just because you're a little hard-up for tail these days!"

For the first time, Stanton had a shocking inkling of the truth.

"Don't bad-mouth yourself into another belting, boy," he warned quietly. "The next one might knock your fool head clean off your shoulders. There's some things I won't take, even from you. Let's get over to the creek before one of the hands sees us like this and douse some sense into you. We both could use a little of that about now."

He retrieved their jackets and grabbed the Missourian by the elbow to steer him toward the seep. Jaime jerked the arm away but went with him. They peeled their shirts and flopped belly-down and thrust their heads and shoulders into the clear little run which an hour before had been fringed with a rime of ice.

The shock bit deep, but it was welcome, anesthetizing cuts and swelling bruises, restoring a sense of balance and a cooler head. They toweled roughly with their shirts before pulling them back on and buttoning their jackets over them against the chill. They sat there on their hams, then, looking at each other.

"Now?" Stanton suggested. "Want to tell me exactly just what in hell this is all about?"

"Damn it, Spence, I'm no kid!" Jaime said, flaring again. "Christ, I got eyes in my head. I seen what's been happening out here. Meeting, when you thought nobody else was around.

Riding together. Laughing. Carrying on."

"Like what?"

"Look, you bastard, don't holy-moly me! I've got respect for 'Mana even if you don't. I been having fits over it ever since that little bitch went out to meet you when you brought the longhorns in and I began to get some notion of what was going on. Last night I'd had it to my ears. I couldn't sleep and I seen a light in the office, so I aimed to have it out with you before it was too late and there was hell to pay all around."

The anger was still there, but there was real anguish in Jaime's eyes.

"You could have at least had the decency to blow out the lamp or hang a blanket over the windows!"

Stanton picked up a twig and traced an aimless pattern before him on the frost-hardened ground.

"Man buys himself a seat like that, uninvited, so to speak, seems like he ought to stick around for the whole show. Pretty hard to tell what it's really all about, otherwise, isn't it?"

"I seen enough."

"I know what you saw. So did I. Not bad, either. Pretty damned wonderful, in fact. But I sure as hell didn't ask for it or expect it. And for what it's worth, I never laid a hand on her."

Stanton narrowly watched Jaime take this. He saw his desire to believe and his effort to do so. But he couldn't make it. Stanton broke the twig between his fingers, cast it aside, and grinned at Jaime.

"Oh, hell, I was tempted all right. I am a horny old bastard. You're right about that. But what I really wanted to do was blister her bottom for her, good and proper. Like I hope I just finished hammering a little sense into your thick head."

"Yeah?" Jaime said suspiciously, still far from convinced. "Then why in hell was she in there so late, alone with you — like that? She crazy or something? Or a goddamned little whore?"

Stanton came to his feet.

"Ask yourself, son. You'll have to admit you've been acting a little peculiar, too."

"That's no answer."

"All right. Let's say she's young and was all upset and mixed up and couldn't think of any other way to convince me. It cost her like hell, too. She's a good girl, Jaime. As good as they come, in her own way, I think."

"Makes even less sense."

"It's simple enough. You see, she's convinced I saved her life when I brought her in from the malpais. Right now, she thinks she's in love with me because of that. Don't laugh, damn it. It's happened to me a time or two before, in case you want to know. Like right now you think you hate my guts. And you're both wrong as hell. But you'll both get over it. If my patience doesn't run out. Come on. Back on the job. We've got a ranch to run."

Jaime began to grin. Stanton smiled to himself. The Missourian's loyalty and devotion to 'Mana was touching and fiercely sincere. He had fresh and painful knots and bruises left on his own body by vengeful hands in proof of that. And he knew that to face him must have taken every ounce of guts and fury Jaime had.

But he had been confusing causes, as the young so often did. It was not for 'Mana Stanton that Jaime had fought the *patrón* of the Corona. However much he had believed it to be so these many weeks, it was not for 'Mana Stanton that Jaime had suffered.

Stanton chuckled enviously. For the first time in this fashion, he was aware of his own years.

They went back to their horses and retrieved their hats and gear and mounted up.

"I suppose I have to tell you," Stanton growled. "You're good with your hands. About as good as I ever had to take on. I wasn't so damned sure there for a bit. But I'm afraid I marked you up a little, too. Better stay away from the house for a few days till you heal up some."

"Now?" Jaime protested. "Like hell!"

Stanton shrugged.

"I can explain to 'Mana. I doubt you can to the girl. Or want to. The truth of it."

Jaime's grin widened.

"Nothing to it. Dabbed a loop on a big long-horn that broke my rig and jerked me off, saddle and all. I'll get Mama Archuleta to put one of her pig-fat and bread poultices on tonight. Good as new, tomorrow. Few marks of character is all."

229

CHAPTER EIGHTEEN

Jaime's story held and he became a familiar about the house again. It was he who now occasionally met Helga Cagle on the range.

Spring came. So did 'Mana's child. A boy, full term, perfect in all respects, as she had promised from the beginning. Labor was brief, the birth easy. Rosa Dominguín proudly presided as midwife. Stanton and Jaime Henry took refuge in the office when Helga and the other women ran them out. It was a long afternoon and they got drunk, big-talking the years to come.

Much annoyed that the good God had wrought the expected miracle ahead of him, Father Frederico arrived two days later from Taos and the child was christened Roberto Ruíz Stanton in memory of 'Mana's father. The holy water was yet damp on the dark infant curls when the cooing women diminished the name to Robertito. It was shortened further to Tito before the Corona heir ceased to cry lustily every time Spencer Stanton's towering figure intruded upon the familiar world of feminine bustle in the nursery.

The short, masculine form pleased Stanton, whose own name had always had an awkward sound in his ears. Bob would have suited him as well for brevity, but as Jaime said, it did not suit the country. So Tito was swiftly accepted by all.

Mother and child prospered. The grass greened. Stock fattened on the new growth. Coats shed out to summer sleekness. From the veranda and upper rooms of the house, the new wealth of the Corona was everywhere apparent, as far as the eye could reach. Stanton knew the long time of waiting was coming to an end.

'Mana grew concerned that Felipe Peralta had not come to pay his respects. Surely he knew that her time was now many weeks past. She feared all was not well with the old man. Stanton doubted this, knowing Abelardo or another would have sent them word, and he counseled patience. In a few more days, Don Felipe arrived. But it was hardly the neighborly social occasion 'Mana anticipated.

He and Abelardo were accompanied by more than twenty others, dons and *rancheros*. The same men of property and influence who had joined Don Felipe in support of Governor Armijo when he had seized control of the province shortly after Stanton's arrival in New Mexico. They had been prepared to fight for their lives then. They were now. And many were plainly none too sure that Spencer Stanton was not their enemy.

Their suspicions were not eased when Chato rode in with a party of armed Utes which considerably outnumbered them, shortly after their own arrival. The haughty young Ute chief visibly eased when he recognized Abelardo and the old don of Mora among them.

"With so many coming this way, we could not tell from the mountains if they were friends, *amigo*," he told Stanton in his sibilant Spanish, "so we came down to see. Since all seems well, we will go, now."

"No, Chato. I'm glad you're here. I think you'd better come in with the rest."

Chato dismounted and moved through the hostile New Mexicans, as much a don as any of them. 'Mana met him at the door, Tito in her arms. He admired the baby extravagantly and followed her into the house. At a nod from Stanton, Amelio led the rest of the Utes off toward the adobes to see that they were fed according to long-standing custom when they visited the Corona. Each carried the rifle without which he would not quit his horse, these days. Don Felipe's friends watched them go with sullen side glances at Stanton.

He understood well enough. The New Mexicans knew he had bought Chato's people these weapons and now supplied them with powder and ball. But these were Indians, oldest of their enemies, and to the Spanish way of thinking — inherited from ancient times — it was treason to arm savages, whatever the justification.

Ignoring the glances, Stanton led his uninvited guests into the big living room. Helga and Jaime brought more chairs and benches from elsewhere in the house. The women withdrew and they all sat down. Don Felipe soberly explained the purpose of their visit.

He had just returned with some of these friends from Santa Fe. Governor Armijo had grave news for them. Texas, as had long been feared, had managed to get herself annexed to the States, joining her cause to that of the Union. Zachary Taylor, general of an army sent to secure the borders of the new state, had met and defeated a Mexican force at Palo Alto, across the Rio Grande from Matamoros, and President Polk had issued a proclamation officially declaring war.

New Mexico was certain to be invaded. General Stephen Kearney was reported already marching his Army of the West down the Santa Fe Trail for that purpose.

The Corona Grant was the farthest outpost in this direction. Potentially a stronghold of much importance. Governor Armijo demanded to know at once where Spencer Stanton's loyalty lay and what could be expected of him when invasion did come. So did his neighbors, here gathered. Would he turn against them with the enemy or would he stand and fight, as they were prepared to do?

This was the division which Stanton had feared and which he had come to believe inevitable. He looked up and saw 'Mana in the shadows at the top of the stairs, Tito hugged protectively in her arms and her face white as she listened to the talk below. He looked back at the dark, for-

233

bidding men before him.

Once again he was being forced to put everything he had gained on the line in a conflict not of his own making and one in which he could win little and risk all. He knew the answer these men wanted. He knew what 'Mana was waiting for him to say. It would be easy and erase most doubts. It would win him friends which might prove invaluable. And it might stand. There were no Yankee soldiers on his grass and might never be. He was far off the road to Santa Fe.

True, he believed the government of his homeland wrong and the motives of many deeply involved suspect if not outright shameless. But a growing belief persisted in him that in the long run — if the folly of head-on battle could somehow be avoided — another change of flags might greatly benefit this contested high country and all within it. He had no choice but to take a difficult middle road and be condemned for it by either side, if that was the way the chips were to fall.

"Some of you will call these *yanqui* words," he said carefully. "But my wife and my friends will know I speak as a New Mexican. For my land and the people who gathered with me on it. For my family and my cattle. Perhaps my life. You and yours, as well.

"I don't speak about justice and right because I don't know. Let those who don't have to do the shooting settle that. But if Mexico has twice been unable to defend herself against the Tex-

234

ans, Mexico City can't defend us against the armies of the United States. And we are too few to stand alone. General Kearney must be allowed to occupy us without resistance. We must accept a new government."

"Treason!" old Simeon Castro cried fiercely. "We are our own men, whatever Mexico City does. You have armed your Indians. If we are too few, we can arm others. With their help, we can turn back ten *yanqui* armies."

Stanton shook his head wearily.

"Tell them, Chato. Tell them what they can expect from the Indians if they attempt to fight."

The Ute slashed a forefinger across his neck in an eloquent cutthroat gesture.

"Not my people," he said. "Not the mountain Utes. We have been friends a long time here, now. But all the rest, I think. The Pueblos, the Navajo, the Apache. Iron Head and his Comanches too, I think. They are old enemies. You are to blame for that and they have not forgotten.

"They will leap on you from behind the minute the first shot is fired. They've only been waiting for the right time, when you are too busy to defend yourselves. They will burn your ranchos, run off your stock, attack your towns. And who will there be to punish them? Not the *yanquis,* my friends. Not the *yanquis.*"

"He speaks the truth," Stanton continued earnestly. "We have a government of one man. He's all there is. I have great personal respect for Manuel Armijo as a friend and a soldier and a governor. But the minute he marches out of Santa Fe to meet the invaders, government will cease to exist.

"Men will die and the Yankees will sweep through New Mexico as conquerors, not as a peaceful occupation force. In the face of resistance their officers will turn them loose to kill, burn, seize what they want by right of conquest. They're that human. That's war as they understand it. You've got to realize that. All of you. And you've got to make the governor realize it as well. Before it's too late and some foolish thing is done."

The room sat sullen and silent. Stanton realized he had not reached them. He could not. The difference was too great. Yet he knew now that he was right. There was no other solution. There could not be. And it was a bitter fact for men of ancient pride to accept.

Felipe Peralta did what he could. He looked slowly about the room, measuring those who had come with him, and shook his head with an old man's weary sadness.

"I don't like these words any more than any of the rest of you, *compañeros*," he said. "But I hear and must listen. I know this man. I do not think they are *yanqui* words. True, that's what he was when he came here. But no more. His mark is on the land. Its mark is on him, as surely as it is on us. As he says, he speaks now as a New Mexican. That's what I will report to the governor."

Stanton saw they wished to discuss his stand

among themselves. He rose and stepped out onto the veranda. Jaime and Chato followed him there.

"They won't go along," Jaime said.

"Some of them won't," Stanton agreed. "That's sure."

"Armijo will listen to them. He'll have to. Mexico City's too far away and he can't afford to make the decision on his own, I'm afraid you're pulling down everything you've built here."

Stanton nodded.

"I know. But I also know old Steve Kearney. If even one *paisano* so much as shakes a fist at that hard-nosed, high-handed bastard, he'll see to it that there isn't an armed Mexican or a single valid Spanish land title left between here and California before he's through. That's his way. The iron heel, if they ask for it."

"And not a damned thing we can do!" Jaime growled.

"Try to hold what we can, whichever way it goes."

"That's better, *amigo*," Chato approved eagerly. "More like Spencer Stanton. Get me enough more guns for the rest of my people and I promise no one will ride into this yard at least, *yanqui* or Mexican."

"No," Stanton answered. "I want you to get your people out of here. Now. Today. Over the mountains. As far as possible. Maybe even up into the Bayou Salado. You haven't had a hunt up there for a long time. And stay until this is

237

over. Settled. Done with. For their own safety."

"A Ute does not turn his back on a friend," Chato protested.

"Damn it, listen to me! Stephen Kearney is the most stubborn Indian fighter in the States. That's how he made his reputation. And he only fights Indians one way. To the finish. If your people killed even one white, *yanqui* or *mexicano,* for whatever reason, he'd call it an uprising and order you hunted down and wiped out to the last man, woman, and child. I can't let you risk that. Go now. The sooner the better."

The Ute looked uncertainly at Jaime. The Missourian nodded soberly.

"Straight from the horse's mouth," he said. "That part, at least. Best get cracking, Chato. *Bueno suerte.*"

The Indian shrugged.

"If you change your mind, show a smoke or a fire, like in the old days," he told Stanton. "I'll leave a messenger behind — and warn him to kill no whites."

Chato crossed to his horse, swung up, and rode down to the adobes to assemble his men. He was barely gone when the New Mexicans filed from the house. With a singular discourtesy for them, they went directly to their horses and mounted without farewell and thanks for courtesy of the Corona roof. Only Felipe Peralta and his *segundo* paused on the veranda.

"I will get your message to the governor as quickly as possible, my friend," the old don said.

"I have no stomach for the task, but I will argue for it because I, too, see no other way. But Manuel Armijo is a headstrong man and I think he has never cared for it that you hold this land and those Texas cattle. And I'm afraid many others will argue against you. I do not know what he will order done. Be on guard."

"Against some of those over there, too," Abelardo added darkly. "There is much hot blood, these days, and I think that they will have you watched. Turn away anyone who comes, *señor*. If they see strangers about, they may decide to take matters into their own hands."

Stanton nodded his thanks and watched his deeply troubled neighbors cross the yard to join their companions. The New Mexicans rode out stiffly, without looking back. Stanton returned to the living room. The empty chairs stared accusingly at him. 'Mana handed Tito to Helga at the top of the stairwell and came down to him.

"I would have fought, Spence," she said quietly.

"I will," he answered. "When I'm sure of the enemy."

"When will you know?"

"When he's in my dooryard."

"It may be too late, then."

"We'll see."

CHAPTER NINETEEN

Stanton and Jaime split the crew to hasten the task and commenced moving the Corona beef into the mountains in small bunches, assigning each to a high, hidden meadow which would hold it till first frost if necessary. It was a couple of weeks earlier than Stanton would have liked, but it had been a mild spring and the mountain season was a little ahead of itself. Security outweighed the fact that some of the high grass was not yet to full stand. So dispersed, it would take anyone without foreknowledge of the location of each bunch an endless time to discover and reassemble the herd.

In ten days the vast expanse of the lower range was nearly as devoid of stock as it had been when Stanton first saw it. All that remained on home graze was the necessary horse cavvy, the little fresh dairy herd, and a few of the culls reserved for the table. The rest of the longhorns and home stock had vanished to casual appearance as though they had never existed.

Taking one drive up the canyon of the Cimarron to scatter it in upland pockets above the Taos trail, Stanton was relieved to discover that Chato had taken his urgent advice. The Utes had abandoned their lower camps and with-drawn over the mountains somewhere into the high, remote headwaters of the Rio Grande.

A little more than three weeks after the delivery of Governor Armijo's ultimatum to the Corona by Felipe Peralta and his friends to the south, the invasion of which they had warned came. A long, Santa Fe-bound line of marching dust along the eastern horizon. In spite of all resolves, Stanton faced a powerful temptation to ride out and make his peace with old Stephen Kearney. Perhaps even to the extent of offering a few head of Corona beef for the general's commissary, necessarily thinned down by the long crossing from the Arkansas.

He supposed their former acquaintance would be remembered without particular malice, and logic told him where the lesser risk lay. Such a move would do much to cement his position and the security of the Corona with Kearney and whatever provisional government he established when the question of military control and sovereignty here was finally settled. As a practical matter, the potential gain was well worth inviting the outrage of a deposed Mexican governor and the hostility of a few neighbors.

But he thought of 'Mana and his infant Mexican son and those friends he had made here whose roots were deep in this land and its history and pride, and he could not betray them, even to this self-benefitting degree. Instead, when it became apparent that the blue column would continue on down the Trail toward Santa Fe without divergence onto the Corona, he rode with Jaime Henry out onto the malpais. They climbed to the corner-mark of the grant on the summit of the cone of Fire Mountain and watched the passage from there.

In the glass the thin military line beneath the marching dust was disconcertingly innocuous in appearance for history on the move. Even with optic aid, distance was too great to be accurate in detail, but Stanton thought the Yankee force could not amount to more than five or six troops of cavalry with possibly half that in foot support. Perhaps a thousand men at full complement. From a military and psychological standpoint, an audacious, inadequate implement with which to attempt seizure and securing of a territory several times larger than most European nations.

"The damned fool!" he growled.

Jaime looked at him curiously.

"General Kearney, if that's who's actually in command down there," Stanton continued. "Cocky old bastard. The professional soldier for you. In too hell of a big hurry to get a shooting war going to field a proper army and a really convincing show of strength. Bucking for more medals and another star. Just plain inviting resistance. Fat chance Don Felipe has of persuading Armijo or anyone else to lay down their arms when they see that's all they're up against!"

"I don't know, Spence," Jaime answered thoughtfully. "It don't look like it worries the

242

general none. Look at the size of his baggage train."

Stanton nodded. He thought that, too, was a measure of Kearney's arrogance and professional confidence. Already nearly six hundred miles from his nearest practical base, the old Indian fighter appeared amply supplied for any march the exigencies'of war forced upon him.

"Hell, carrying that much support along with him, he could make it clean to Mexico City if he had to," Jaime continued. "If they don't cut him down, somehow."

"Or California, even," Stanton agreed grimly. "God knows he's got plenty of room to work in."

With infuriating, frustrated concern, Stanton thought that he could already write this page as it would be bound into history. He did not think it would greatly affect the continued existence of the Corona, one way or another. Different forces would be involved there when the time came. But he was now sure that his arguments to Don Felipe and the other dons to the south had been useless. Their pride would not let them give up in the face of no greater apparent threat than this, no matter what common sense and a decent concern for their own people might counsel.

They could not understand that in spite of the lightness of his force, Kearney would prevail in the end simply because he had behind him, however distant, the enormous strength of a powerful and vengeful nation whose only end in battle had always been victory. They could not comprehend that implacable strength because they had never beheld it. They could not see it before them now and would be unable to grasp the futility of resistance until the first shot was fired and it was too late.

Von Clausewitz and the grand strategists notwithstanding, this was the calumny of war. Command was necessarily fallible to the top echelon and mistakes inevitable. Military engagement was the most imprecise of sciences, at best. And so men died needlessly, without accomplishment.

Stanton glared at the distant column under its dust. Less than two days to the south, beyond the great rock of Wagonmound, there was a small settlement of *paisano* farmers at a place called The Meadows, where the Trail swung west for its transit of the mountains. It was the first New Mexican settlement the present line of invasion would encounter. Some gesture of resistance might be made there, but he doubted it. Governor Armijo was a more than competent soldier himself, and the country there was too open, the terrain too favorable to the intruding enemy.

Just as there was no other practical road to Santa Fe, there was only one place to attempt a defensive stand with some hope of surprise and the advantage of a superior position. This was in Apache Canyon on the slope of Glorieta Pass, almost within gun-sound of the capital itself. If Armijo and the *ricos* who counseled him elected to turn out the *paisanos* to contest the Yankee advance, it would be there.

In any event, he had done what he could for those beyond his own boundaries and must now look to himself. The time was close and the news would be fast-traveling, even to the distant Corona. Stanton had seen enough.

"Come on," he said to his *segundo*. "Let's get home."

He started toward his horse. Jaime's voice turned him back.

"Wait a minute, Spence. Look at this —"

The Missourian handed over the glass and Stanton put it to his eye. A body of horsemen perhaps a dozen strong had detached itself from the moving column at right angles and was riding due west along the southern edge of the malpais. He watched them in silence for a moment, the residual hackles of an ancient instinct rising along the back of his neck.

"See how they're riding?" Jaime said. "That bunch are sure as hell no pony soldiers."

Stanton nodded and collapsed the glass with a decisive snap.

"Civilians," he agreed. "Guerrillas. Riding Kearney's coattails. I should have known that's the way they'd come. Get back to the house. Pull everybody in and fort up. Maybe for a long stay. Keep a twenty-four-hour watch and every gun loaded. Shoot anybody who rides in."

"How about you? Where are you going?"

"Same place they're headed. Mora. To hunt

them down before they do me. And I hope to hell I'm in time!"

"The big red Texican you took the longhorns from? You sure it's him?"

"Bypassed us, didn't they? It's the way he'd work. Cut us off from the south before doubling back to close in. Probably with Kearney's blessings, too. A good officer can afford to be generous for a little unofficial guerrilla help as long as it doesn't cost him and confuses the enemy."

Stanton paused, frowning.

"What bothers me is he knows where he's going. He's got somebody with him who knows the country."

"And better than ten to one odds," Jaime protested. "Christ, Spence, you're a big man, but if it's who you think it is and they're after what you think they are, you can't do it alone."

"Just who in the hell am I going to get to help — 'Mana and the baby, maybe? Helga? The women and kids at the adobes? Think I can wait for them to come to me and risk that? Get moving, damn it!"

Stanton was riding the big dappled stallion he had commandeered on the Canadian from Heggie Duncan. The powerful animal was the fastest and hardest-bottomed on the Corona, and Stanton knew every inch of the ground over which he rode, so there was no lost motion. But the party of horsemen from the invading Yankee column had a shorter distance to cover to reach Felipe Peralta's Rancho Mora and a hopeless lead on him.

He had no more idea whether Don Felipe had returned from his mission to Santa Fe than he did what decision Governor Armijo and his advisors had reached, but he was concerned for the old don's safety. No matter how the military conquest of New Mexico went — and he was sure conquest was Kearney's order or at least his intent — there would be great need later for men of the Mexican *ranchero*'s wisdom and patience. His people would face a difficult time at best.

Stanton had no doubt Heggie Duncan was among those men who had quit Kearney's column. He had no doubt of their intentions. He knew he was their ultimate objective. The Corona and its cattle. To cut him off from support, he knew they would attempt to at least neutralize any force at Mora. A wipeout and full-scale plundering would be more likely, if Abelardo and the Mora *vaqueros* failed to stand them off.

He was still deeply troubled by the apparent fact that the guerrillas had the lay of the land and the relationship between Mora and the Corona so pat. Duncan, a stranger, his first time into this country, could know nothing of either. And then suddenly he understood. Helga Cagle's brothers. Or one of them, at least.

He remembered Abelardo's account of running them off Peralta land. They were the only Yankees who had been on both ranches and knew the layout and setup. Now they had returned. In spite of 'Mana's warning and Jaime's and Chato's orders. With the red Scottish giant who called himself Heggie Duncan. Stanton swore under his breath, his concern for those at Mora sharply rising.

It was already dark when he rode his hard-breathing horse onto Don Felipe's land. He came in from the north as he had once before when Mora had been under siege, dismounting behind a small hill which overlooked the Peralta house and hid his approach from view. He climbed to the crest of this and looked down into the compound. Lamplight glowed hospitably in Don Felipe's windows and those of the bunkhouse at the lower end of the yard. All seemed serene in the moonless silence of the evening.

For a moment he wondered if it was all a figment of his imagination, an unreasonable jump to conclusions unwarranted by the facts. Heggie Duncan and the Cagles were not among those who had split off from Kearney's column. Those men had no knowledge of Spencer Stanton or designs upon his land and cattle. And they had not been bound for Mora at all. There was no danger here. He had made a hard and punishing ride for nothing and he had unnecessarily alarmed 'Mana and the others at the Corona by his suspicions and fears and the precautions he had forced upon them.

Then warning instinct surfaced again. Dogs

always roved the Mora yard. The wind was at his back and they would have already sensed his presence. Yet there was no sound from below. The silence was ominous. He returned to his horse, swiftly unsaddled, and hobbled it on thick grass near a small seep, knowing it would not stray far from the water and so inadvertently betray his presence.

Reclimbing the hill, rifle in hand, he started down the other side, careful to dislodge nothing underfoot. Even small sounds carried a surprising distance at night in this high air. ·

He found the first dog well out from the yard, where it had apparently coursed to investigate. He thought it had been roped and its neck broken by a quick set of the roper's horse. Another was nearer the corrals. Its throat had been cut. Both quick kills, with no chance of more than a startled yelp of protest and then sudden silence. He supposed a similar fate had met any others.

This had meaning. If there was need to silence the dogs, not only were the guerrillas here, but they had not arrived too much ahead of him. They, too, had reached Mora after nightfall and approached by stealth. He moved on silently, trying to make up his mind whether to try the main house or the bunkhouse first.

Suddenly the dust was wet underfoot. He knelt and fingered it, recognizing the faint, warm smell. Blood. A trail of blood where an injured man had dragged himself across the ground. He followed the track. Toward the main house, because that was where it led. But it soon ended. Skirting the woodpile, Stanton heard a man's painfully labored breathing ahead. He froze, then eased down behind the ax-scarred chopping stump until he could pinpoint the source of the sound.

He thought the man lay against a stack of rounds sawed for splitting, five or six yards away. He carefully leveled the rifle across the stump, knowing that if he was discovered, the long gun would have to be the first discarded. When he was sure he had his target on mark if it became necessary to fire, he took a calculated risk.

"*Quién es?*" he whispered softly.

The answer came with difficulty in an even softer whisper, in which he sensed relief.

" 'Lardo. Francisco — ?"

Stanton eased gratefully.

"Your neighbor, *amigo.*"

The injured man's response was a deep sigh and Stanton knew he understood. He moved swiftly to him.

Abelardo lay on his belly with his face in the litter of wood chips on the ground. Stanton gently turned him over. He had a large, wet wound on one side, just under the ribcage. It was bleeding copiously.

"*El patrón* —" he breathed urgently.

"You first, before you bleed to death."

Stanton could not tell if there was any hope for the man, but working by feel alone, he swiftly packed his kerchief into the wound in an attempt to control the bleeding.

"Only Francisco and Edmundo were here when they came." Abelardo winced with pain. "The rest are in the mountains. *Bastardos!* That was a big knife they put in me. Who are they? *Yanqui* soldiers, already?"

"Old friends," Stanton answered grimly. "Paying a return visit. Hang tough and don't try to move. I'll be back."

Abelardo clutched at him.

"The *patrón, señor* — if he is — if he can no longer tell you himself — there is something you must know. Look in his desk. It is important. Look in his desk. *Entiéndele?*"

"*Entiéndolo,*" Stanton agreed.

He disengaged the clutching hand and moved away from the Mora *segundo*, backtracking a little to get clear of the chips about the woodpile. On smooth yard dirt he slipped his boots and resumed toward the house in stocking feet. Half way across, the front door swung open, stabbing a shaft of yellow light into the stygian yard which nearly caught him in its beam. Zeke Cagle came out along it from the veranda, unbuttoning his fly, and stepped aside into the darkness to relieve himself.

Stanton's teeth sucked back from his lips as he remembered the scarring look of trembling abhorrence in 'Mana's eyes when she finally told him how this bastard had tried to use her when she still had blood on her hands from saving his brother's life. Keeping clear of the shaft of light,

251

he ran lightly forward, moving so fast that the man had not yet started to puddle before he was onto him. He could have dropped the son of a bitch soundlessly where he stood stupidly in surprise with his penis in his hand, but satisfaction was worth the risk of outcry.

Swinging the barrel of his rifle in a short, vicious horizontal arc, Stanton struck the Cagle sharply across the throat an inch or two above the collarbone, crushing and paralyzing the voice box. Breath and blood belched from his mouth in a paroxysm of agony, but no sound, as Stanton had intended.

Dropping the rifle, he seized the half-stunned Cagle by the hair with both hands, forcing his head far back, and rammed a knee hard up under the open fly of his pants. Cagle shuddered and would have doubled forward but could not. The knee chopped up again and again, pistoning remorselessly, until Stanton felt the belly wall go like the shell of a pumpkin.

The man sagged. Stanton stepped back and hit him twice in the face as he fell, once from either side. They were terrible, smashing swings, with the full weight of his body behind them. The second unhinged the jaw, driving it far around to one side. Cagle sprawled limply and did not move. Still it was not enough. Stanton seized the hair again to jerk him up for more, but the head rolled loosely on a flaccid neck and he realized it was over. A last orgasm of death.

CHAPTER TWENTY

Stanton drew a deep breath and reason returned. There was no alarm. From this position he could now hear the rise and ebb of the voices of several men in normal converse beyond the closed door of the bunkhouse. It was impossible to tell how many. But the sound told him they believed themselves without further opposition.

Ahead was a subdued clatter from the main house, as though small items of furniture were being shifted about. Leaving his rifle where it lay, Stanton scooped up Zeke Cagle's handgun and found it fully capped. Thrusting it into his belt opposite his own, he slid swiftly onto the veranda of the main house, staying wide of the shaft of light from the open front door.

Risking silhouette against the unglazed, shuttered opening, he peered through the slats of a small, shoulder-high window. The time-mellowed, comfortable graciousness of Felipe Peralta's living room was a shambles.

Furniture had been overturned, kicked out of the way. Cabinets had been torn open, shelves stripped, and their contents carelessly flung broadcast. Matt and Lew Cagle were burrowing impatiently in the debris, prying into anything that yet remained unopened. Sitting upright in a high-backed chair beside the door to her kitchen was Josefina, Don Felipe's housekeeper. She seemed frozen in a catatonic trance of stupefied, slack-featured fear and horror.

Her gaze was fixed across the room on Don Felipe's figure, back to the window through which Stanton peered, slumped in a similar chair and almost completely screened from Stanton's view by the high back. The old don's slender-fingered, veined brown hands gripped the armrests without tension or movement.

Lew Cagle, seemingly completely recovered from the bullet Stanton had put into him at Taylor Springs, straightened near the old man. Cagle held in his hands a delicate, intricately-patterned ceramic Pueblo jar to which the master Indian potter had fitted a marvelously graceful and snug lid. Cagle jerked this off hopefully and saw the contents: two or three dozen black, crooked, unsymmetrical Mexican cigars which Stanton remembered as among the best he had ever smoked.

"Oh, God damn it!" Cagle exploded.

He flung the jar from him and it crashed against the fireplace in a spray of fragments. He wheeled on Don Felipe's chair and leaned forward to grip its half-hidden occupant's shoulder with vindictive insistence.

"The gold," he demanded harshly. "Money. *Moneda. Dinero.* Where the hell is it? You live like this, you got to have pots of it around."

He broke off and stepped back stupidly as the brown hands slid without resistance from the armrests and the figure of Don Felipe Peralta tumbled limply from the chair to the floor. Stanton could see, now, what had riveted Josefina's horrified gaze. The sightless eyes were wide open, staring accusingly, even defiantly, still, at the roof *vigas* above. A little thickening blood had trickled from one nostril and the corner of the mouth. The features were puffed and bruised by many hard-palmed slapping blows.

"Hey, Matt," Lew called, "I think the old bastard's croaked on us!"

Matt Cagle backed from a tall cabinet he was researching and looked across at the body on the floor.

"Oh, Christ!" he swore.

"I told you Zeke was laying it on too hard."

"Quit whining," Matt snapped. He turned on Josefina. "We'll damned well get it out of her. She's got to know where it's hid. Give me your knife. These greasers got no guts. Cold steel scares the shit out of them."

Stanton waited for no more. He came in through the door like a cat, his own belt gun in one hand and Zeke Cagle's in the other, not caring now if he exposed himself to light. Both men were leaning over Josefina where she sat frozen in her chair. Matt Cagle already had the point of his brother's knife a quarter of an inch into the flesh of her heavy breast, wickedly increasing the pressure with little twisting motions.

"Talk, you bitch!" he was demanding. *"El oro,* savvy? *Adonde?"*

Stanton knew that Josefina saw him behind her tormentors and that she recognized him. But by not even the flicker of an eye did she betray his presence. And the Cagles scorned Mexican courage!

He raised the heavy barrels of both guns high and brought them down together with every ounce of force in him. Both skulls shattered simultaneously and both bodies sprawled across Josefina's lap. So he kept the promise 'Mana had made to Helga Cagle's brothers if they ever reentered New Mexico.

Wheeling, he darted back to the door. That of the bunkhouse across the yard remained closed. He shut the veranda door, cutting off the shaft of light across the yard, returned to Josefina, and dumped the limp carrion befouling her to the floor.

"No sound," he warned.

She nodded.

"Are you all right?"

She touched the place where the knife had punctured her skin, but nodded again. He smiled at her and patted her cold, limp hand.

"Good, *mamasita.* Soon it will be over. But I need some help. A ball of string — twine — anything."

He helped her up and she went to her room beyond the kitchen. While she was gone, he stripped the last two Cagles of their guns. She returned with a big hank of hard-spun, undyed wool. He took it.

"There will be shooting," he warned. "Stay here. Quiet."

Once more she nodded, saying nothing. He saw the faith and hope in her eyes. He started for the door, then turned back. He remembered the four fresh graves on the Canadian beside which he had once before faced Heggie Duncan in showdown, and he hated to spare the weapon, but he handed Josefina one of the Cagle guns. She gripped it firmly.

"For you. If I don't come back and you need it. *Comprende?*"

For answer, she cocked the weapon efficiently and laid it ready across her lap. He gripped her shoulder and let himself out into the night with the two remaining Cagle guns and his own, closing the door behind him.

He picked up his rifle beside Zeke Cagle's body and went on to the woodpile, wincing at chip-splinters under his stockinged feet as he approached.

" 'Lardo — ?"

"*Sí, señor. Aquí.*"

He found the wounded man and knelt beside him.

"*Como está, ahora?*"

"I live. *El patrón —*"

"*Muerte.* So are the Cagles, now. All that are left are the big, red Scot from the Canadian and some others in the bunkhouse. No more than seven or eight, I think. Can you shoot?"

"*Como siempre,*" the wolf of Mora said grimly. "And I won't miss. I promise you that."

Stanton helped Abelardo roll over to a prone position, saw that he had a good angle into the bunkhouse dooryard, and gave him another of the Cagle guns.

"I'll start it. Wait for me. Wherever. If they come out shooting, knock the sons of bitches over."

"*Bueno suerte, señor.*"

Tucking one of the sawed rounds of firewood ready for splitting stacked near where the Mora *segundo* lay under his arm and carrying his rifle, Stanton moved swiftly back into the yard. He lined himself up carefully on a direct line from the bunkhouse to the main house veranda, lashed the rifle to the firewood round for a rest and anchor, and sighted in gut-high on the bunkhouse door.

He fastened the end of Josefina's hank of tight, hardspun yarn to the rifle trigger, threading it through the guard for a sure angle to pull. Cocking the weapon, he moved away, carefully paying out the black yarn behind him.

He picked a spot at a corner pillar of the mainhouse veranda. The thick adobe column provided cover and gave him a good angle of crossfire with Abelardo's position, at close enough range for both to be as effective as possible under such unfavorable shooting conditions. But before he could get set to his satisfaction and issue his planned challenge to the occupants of the bunkhouse, the slack string of yarn in his fingers jerked suddenly taut and snapped, somewhere out in the darkness.

The pre-sighted rifle fired, but the violence of the tug on the triggering string jerked the weapon askew. Its charge roared off prematurely into the night sky, wasting one of the precious shots available to him and risking betrayal of his whole plan.

Stanton heard a startled imprecation out along the line of slack yarn and he realized at once what must have happened. While he was in the main house with Josefina, a man must have emerged from the bunkhouse on a night errand, by the direction, across to the outhouse. While the man was occupied there, he had himself emerged from the main house and set his trap. On his way back to the bunkhouse, the man had inadvertently hooked a boot toe on the trip string.

He heard the man start to run but could not see him. Then the bunkhouse door was jerked open from within, releasing a shaft of welcome light, and men poured out to investigate the rifle shot in what they had believed was a secured and peaceful yard. Unlike his attack on the Cagles, who had long since forfeited any right to so civilized a gesture, Stanton had intended to give those within the bunkhouse a fair if somewhat exaggerated warning. But he had no choice, now.

He commenced firing swiftly but unhurriedly. His first target was the man running back across the yard. He dropped him as he almost collided with his companions as they poured into the lamplit dooryard and before he could communicate his cause for alarm to any of them.

At the first muzzle flash of his weapon, Abelardo opened up from the woodpile. He made good his promise not to miss, taking one man and then another.

Stanton saw the huge bulk of Heggie Duncan but did not have a clear shot and he broke the back of a man intervening as their guns began to answer Abelardo and himself. It was good shooting in such bad light, even if the targets were tight-packed and milling momentarily in confused silhouette against the lighted doorway. Then it was abruptly over.

Only Heggie Duncan and two others remained on their feet and they dived back though the doorway, slamming the heavy panel shut behind them. But one carried lead with him. Stanton was not sure whether from the wolf of Mora's gun or his own.

The lamp within was quickly snuffed. Sudden silence settled over the yard. Stanton raised his voice.

"Spencer Stanton, Duncan. The Corona. We have you. Show sense. Light your lamp."

There was a momentary pause, then the lamp wick was touched alight again.

"Leave your iron behind and come out slow,"

Stanton continued. "Bring your lamp with you."

The door cautiously opened. A man emerged uncertainly, blinking in the wavering glare of the lamp he carried before him. He was unarmed and exceedingly careful to show it. Heggie Duncan's great hulk followed, also beltless. They stopped beside the bodies sprawled in the dooryard.

"Where's the other one?" Stanton called across from the veranda.

Duncan tilted his head toward the bunkhouse behind him.

"In there," the big Scot said harshly. "He won't be coming out. You got him, too."

"Throw those other guns inside and shut the door."

Duncan obeyed woodenly. He came back to the lamp and glared across the yard.

"Damn your eyes, Stanton," he said raggedly. "I've killed men, too. Maybe more than my share. As was necessary. But never like this! Never unless I could see their faces and they mine. Never until they damned well knew why and had their say, by God! You're a bloody bastard. May Auld Clootie make you answer in the fires of hell for this!"

"Both of you come over here, easy, and I'll answer right now," Stanton called.

Duncan and the man with the lamp crossed warily toward the house. As they passed, lamp glow revealed Zeke Cagle's mauled and broken body in the dirt of the yard. They stepped around it but said nothing. Stanton stepped from the shadows to meet them as they reached the veranda. He flung the door open ahead of them. They uncertainly entered.

Josefina was still in her chair, with the other two Cagles at her feet. She raised her cocked pistol in quick alarm but limply returned it to her lap when she saw Stanton. Heggie Duncan stepped past the man with the lamp and a pair of strides into the ransacked room. His eyes traveled from the Cagles to the body of Don Felipe Peralta, not missing in passing the knife at Josefina's feet and the fresh blood on her flesh and the bodice of her dress. Duncan's features hardened and he nodded.

"You've answered enough," he said.

"Now it's your turn, Duncan," Stanton told him inflexibly.

The man stiffened.

"You'd na be thinking Heggie Duncan had a hand in this!" he protested.

"You're here."

"Aye, man. By right. There's a war about, if you've na heard. An army on the march. Bellies to be fed. I'm here by General Kearney's orders. On contract to buy beef for his quartermaster. From the enemy. To support a siege of Santa Fe, if they stand against the general there. Great God, not for this!"

The big man's usually hard and implacable eyes were pleading.

"Not Heggie Duncan!" he repeated. "These

filthy swine —" He prodded Matt Cagle's body with the toe of his boot. "They knew where plenty of Mexican beef could be had in these parts, so I made agreement on shares with them at the River. They brought us here."

His glance toward Don Felipe's body and the blood on Josefina's bosom again.

"Bloody damned butchers!"

"Why here?" Stanton demanded coldly. "The bastards knew where I was. And you knew I had all the cattle you'd need for your contract."

"Aye," Duncan agreed. "We talked on it. That's a fact, right enough. They claimed they had a score to settle with you, too, and they wanted to try you first. But you and I, man, we'd locked horns before and I wanted na part of more except on my own choosing. Not until this fighting's over and I'd had my profit from the contract and I had a chance to make sure I stood well enough with the general when he took over down here. I'm na so reckless a man as you may think."

He paused, shaking his head at the destruction before him.

"This I dinna ken. It was no part of the bargain. We had to get his hands, three of them, because they were trying to get us and we couldn't tell how many more there might be. But the old man understood how war is. As fine a gentleman as you'd ever see. And reasonable. He agreed to sell me what I would need. Without even hard words.

263

"I left these two and their brother with him and the woman to keep watch until morning, is all. That's the whole truth of it. Why'd they do this? Tell me."

"Gold," Stanton said bluntly. "Money. A mistake Yankee strangers always make with these people. They have a lot of land and they have been here a long time and they live well. Like this. So they must have much gold. But they don't. Any of them. They have no need for it, no use for it, and no respect for what it stands for in most Yankee minds. Take Don Felipe in and put him in his own bed. He's at least entitled to that dignity for the rest of the night. Josefina will show you where."

The housekeeper took one of the lamps and sadly led the way. Heggie Duncan and his remaining man obediently and respectfully lifted the shrunken body of the last of the Peraltas and carried it from the room. Stanton absently kicked through the debris on the floor, righted a drawer which had been yanked from Don Felipe's desk, and began returning its contents. A piece of stiff vellum, folded and sealed in wax with the Peralta crest, caught his eye.

The name of Spencer Stanton was inscribed in elegant old Spanish script beneath the seal. He broke the wax wafer and opened the folds. The single sheet was also written in Felipe Peralta's firm hand and over his formal signature. Stanton's eyes suddenly misted in spite of himself as he saw it was a simple testament, bequeathing Rancho Mora and all upon it. "— to Roberto Ruíz Stanton, my godson."

'Mana was New Mexican. He thought that once again she could accept the death of another old friend. It was a necessity of living. But this would break her heart.

Josefina and the two men returned. He sent the housekeeper across to the bunkhouse with a lamp and a basket to retrieve the guns Duncan had been forced to abandon there. The men he ordered to carry out the Cagles and to bring Abelardo up from the woodpile, warning them to approach him carefully, using his own name for reassurance, then to dig a grave behind the corrals for those in the yard.

"See here, now, Stanton!" Heggie Duncan protested with displeasure. "I'll do my penance where it's due, and glad enough, but damned if I'll be errand-boy for any man, even when he's got me by the balls. Whistle in your own boys. They made that meat out there. Let them bury it."

"I don't have any to whistle in," Stanton said quietly.

The big Scot stared at him incredulously.

"What the hell do you mean, no men?" he demanded. "All those guns out there —"

"Me and Don Felipe's foreman. The wounded man at the woodpile."

Duncan gaped, then began to laugh ruefully.

"Oh, lordy, lordy, lordy!" he moaned. "You've had me again. Twice to Heggie Duncan with my guns in my hands and more than enough good men at my back! By the brass-bound butt of Beelzebub's favorite whore, I'll na risk it another time. You've had your last scurry with me. Maybe we can not be friends, right out. That may be too much. But I promise you this, man, I'll keep to my side of the street from here on out if you'll keep to yours. And a promise made, I keep."

Stanton eyed him a long moment in silence, recognizing the big man's earnestness and essential honesty. He, too, did not know if friendship would prove possible in time, or even desirable, but neither did he want Heggie Duncan for an enemy again. The respect was mutual.

"So do I, Duncan," he said finally. "It seems a fair man's deal."

They shook hands there in the lamplight. A firm, straightforward grip with no test of strength in it. Each had the measure of the other in that, at least.

Duncan's remaining man stared uncomprehendingly at them. The Scot turned to him.

"Come on," he said. "It's to the woodpile for us. Then a pair of shovels. We've got some planting to do. And bring a lamp. I've had enough dark for one night."

Daylight proved that Abelardo's wound was not as severe as Stanton had feared. He rested comfortably in the straightened house with Josefina to ease her grief by fussing over him.

Stanton and Heggie Duncan buried Don Felipe on the knoll behind the house where stood the markers of the long line of other Peraltas who had lived and died on Rancho Mora before him.

Stanton built a big fire near the woodpile and threw on great chunks of tallow. The greasy smoke climbed high into the clear and motionless air and the rest of the Mora *vaqueros* came down from the mountains in response. Saddened, life resumed on the rancho.

Three days later, Stanton rode north with the big Scot and his remaining man. Long before they were into the yard and she was into her husband's arms, Duncan's presence told 'Mana all she needed to know after a long and agonizingly anxious vigil. Stanton's return and the absence of three other men who had been brothers laid to rest Helga Cagle's last fear. She embraced him, but as Jaime did, with relief and joy and respectful affection. Her heart was in it but her body no longer was. He felt deep relief of his own that this had also passed.

Jaime and the crew brought down a hundred and fifty head of market beef from one of the high summer pastures and they sold them to Heggie Duncan at a fair price which left him room for profit on his contract. Amelio proudly rolled out the chuckwagon. Jaime chose four others and they set out with the big Scot and his cattle for the Santa Fe Trail and the tracks of General Kearney's invading army. So life resumed on the Corona, as well.

Jaime and the crew returned with momentous news from Santa Fe and a message through Sol Wetzel. Manuel Armijo had heeded Spencer Stanton's advice, after all. He had evacuated the ancient Palace of the Governors, disbanded and sent home his provincial guards, and withdrawn to his family properties at Albuquerque. Kearney had marched unhindered through Apache Canyon and occupied the New Mexican capital without firing a shot.

The general was preparing to march on to California. Through Wetzel he sent a message to the master of the Corona. He had learned how influential the Yankee rancher had been in persuading the Mexican governor to make his humane and wise no-contest decision. Kearney was anxious to form a suitable provisional government under the flag of the United States before resuming his march and would welcome Spencer Stanton's presence and assistance in the capital. So Stanton must ride again. But he was pleased at the honor and the knowledge he could now afford to go. All was in order here.

He stood with his back to the fireplace in the big room of the house he was building for his wife and her child and watched 'Mana nursing the baby. His satisfaction was deep as he looked at his son. He had become what he intended. He was a big *ranchero* in this new land which was also so old. But there was already a bigger one in this house. In the suckling infant in 'Mana's arms, by an old man's desire to live on in this way, was a union of the Corona and Rancho Mora.

No man ever died completely. No man ever built alone.